I Will Go Barefoot
All Summer for You

I Will Go Barefoot
All Summer for You

KATIE LETCHER LYLE

J.B. LIPPINCOTT COMPANY
Philadelphia and New York

U.S. Library of Congress Cataloging in
Publication Data

Lyle, Katie Letcher, birth date
  I will go barefoot all summer for you.

  SUMMARY: Chronicles the experiences of a
thirteen-year-old girl during the summer she falls
in love for the first time.
  I. Title.
PZ7.L9797Ig   [Fic]   72-13700
ISBN-0-397-31445-0

For Louis Rubin

By cool Siloam's shady rill
   The lily must decay;
The rose that blooms beneath the hill,
   Must shortly fade away.
      "By Cool Siloam's Shady Rill"
   Bishop Reginald Heber (1783–1826)

*I Will Go Barefoot
All Summer for You*

1

"Toby Bright's coming," announced Rose, somewhere beyond the first of June. Rose: my third cousin: Frances's mother: rather too fat, with graying hair and skin to match: she put one finger in between her camel-colored teeth and her gums to dislodge something. Bacon gristle.

And that's the way it started, with just that name. The possibility of Toby Bright's being a boy was interesting. Its sound was like hemp twine, the shiny, pale gold kind. Having looked forward to vacation all winter long, it was disappointing that nothing in particular seemed to be happening.

I had lived with Charlie, Rose, and Frances for two years, ever since my Aunt Dorothy died. Frances was about my age and my third cousin once removed.

I had written a hillbilly song entitled, "I Fell Down and Broke My Heart." I thought it was really good, but Frances said that my title did not make any sense at all; it ought to be "I Fell and Broke My Heart." My own opinion was that my title swung more and she was missing the point. I would have sent it in (Charlie sometimes said quietly about a joke we'd made up or a picture one of us had painted: "That's good. You ought to send it in"), but I didn't know where. Charlie was like that, always kind. Sometimes I wished he was my father instead of Frances's.

The only thing so far to recommend this summer was that I had got my picture into the paper without even trying. I tried all the time to think of ways to do it, and then one day out of the blue sky it happened. I was sent by Rose to the drugstore on our trip to town. ("Glycerin and rose water lotion, Jessie, four ounces; a tube of zinc oxide; and a box of Coughettes. Can you please remember that?" Rose was annoyed at me in advance, since she was pretty sure I would probably not remember it all.) I had had to walk by the Seventh-Day Adventist Church where something interesting was going on. Hailed by Eugene Sayle, the only one of them I knew (who among other things was not allowed to go to the movies at all or to read funny papers), I crossed the street to find out what was happening. I was about to ask when a grown voice, irritable as sandpaper in the heat of Main Street that wavered above the sidewalk, commanded everyone to be quiet and assemble on the steps and watch the birdie. I did, smiling as hard as I could right into the sun, trying not to squint.

My picture showed up in next day's paper, very clear, taller even than Eugene, taller in fact than anyone else, and blonder too, grinning smack in the middle of the back row. My name was in the caption, supplied, I guessed, by Eugene, as a member of the Rose of Sharon Seventh-Day Adventist Church

Daily Vacation Bible and Play School. Rose was not happy. She was very serious about our being Episcopalians, and so I had not told about meeting Eugene when I returned from the drugstore. I had forgotten the zinc oxide, of course, but had remembered she wanted something in a tube and so brought toothpaste. I hadn't thought she would be interested in any adventure tales and it was a hot day.

I was very excited about the picture and used my allowance on two more copies of the paper; also Frances was greenly jealous: "That's the stupidest picture I ever saw. I am sure glad I wasn't along."

Just now, I noticed that, whoever Toby Bright was, Frances's reaction seemed excessive.

"Oh, *him!* Oh, *ugh!* Oh, *awful!*" she moaned, toppling over sideways in her seat. She had never acted that way before, but could generally be counted on to be original. She had said "him." If it wasn't a dog or a man, it had to be a boy. She made her best face, the one Rose hated, squeezing her nose all out of shape, misshaping her mouth, her tongue hanging halfway down her chin; the entire expression made even better by gagging noises. Probably it wasn't a dog or a man because she wouldn't have got that excited over either.

"Stop that!" commanded Rose, dunking a limp cinnamon bun into her muddy coffee, though we were not allowed to do that with milk and cookies.

"Who?" I wanted to know.

"Sit UP," said Rose.

"I'm *sitting.*"

"*Frances.*"

"I'm not *talking* to him."

"Who?"

"Yes, you are *too* going to talk to him."

"W-H-O?" I spelled out very loudly.

"Over my dead body," Frances said grimly.

"Frances's cousin," Rose said, at last turning to me. "A Very Nice Boy." A look warned Frances not to try anything else. "Very Nice" capitalized itself into bright letters in my head. I knew to regard comments like that as probable lies. All things considered, Very Nice just about canceled out Boy. Long before thirteen I learned that Very Nice People were the very people who were never nice. Wonderful people were even worse. They were dull.

"My cousin too?" I asked in the middle of swallowing my brown-red vitamin pill. (One of my chiefest talents: I could do it without water. Frances couldn't, but she'd been working on it. One day she took twenty of them trying to learn, and made me swear I wouldn't tell.)

"You can *have* him," she said. "I'm leaving for Dubuque. That's in Iowa."

"*I* knew *that*."

"No," Rose answered my question. "Charlie's sister's son. No kin to you." (I was to hear those words like an echo all summer long: No—kin—to—you.) Saying that, Rose got up, leaning heavily on the table, her arms like dough even to the color; she collected some dishes and started to the kitchen. Her skin looked as though, if you punched it, it ought to stay punched in. When she was gone I drank the coffee left in her saucer, partly because I liked it and was not allowed to drink it, but mostly so my growth would be stunted. Already I was five feet six, two inches taller than Frances, who was ten and a half months older; and worse, I was miles taller than the tallest boy in our class, Bobby Lowenstein.

I removed my gum from its hiding place under the table.

Chewing gum was a lot easier than brushing my teeth, and besides, I was using it as a sort of scientific experiment. I had chewed the same piece of gum, Juicy Fruit, with only four additions, for one hundred and three days now, and my aim was forever. I secretly called it "perpetual gum," and could visualize in an instant the black newspaper headlines: MISS JESSIE PRESTON HAS CHEWED THE SAME PIECE OF GUM FOR FIFTY YEARS; or, WORLD-FAMOUS GUM-CHEWING CHAMP DOES IT AGAIN. I was only sorry about the twelve and two-thirds years wasted before I had thought of it.

As soon as I could get Frances alone, I asked her about Toby Bright. She was not particularly subtle.

"He is stupid and ugly and I hate him," she said, and followed her comment with one of her famous sound effects. "He likes *bugs*," she added. I had to admit it sounded bad. But I had come upon her unsuspecting and unexpected.

"Why are you putting on lipstick?" I asked.

She shrugged. "No reason. I just happen to like the taste."

We hadn't worn lipstick for a couple of years and the old tubes with names like Tea Rose, Summer Honey, Pink Lightning, and Plum Passion were grainy and dry when we came across them. There was a time, though, when we were lipstick experts. We were younger then, and I still lived with Dorothy. Lack of money was the big problem in the days of our lipstick research, so most of our forty-two were acquired the day we were taken as guests to the community swimming pool. We raided every single basket in the women's locker room and went home that day with sixteen lipsticks each.

Although I read the newspaper carefully for a long time, to my sorrow the terrible theft was never mentioned. After that, Frances and I discussed the comparative smoothness of various shades of lipstick and the flavors of different brands. We sent off twenty-five cents for a book on the art of kissing in which we read that you held your head sideways to kiss, but must always remember to blot your lipstick beforehand. The only thing we couldn't figure out was about breathing. We left our blots everywhere, and practiced kissing on trees, fences, a collie named Lady who lived next door to Dorothy and me, even on each other.

After school in the afternoons we pledged not to fight until the next day (at school we fought all day because she made higher grades, but I got more reports of boys who wanted to dance with me in Music; the teacher called on her more, but I made a higher grade on the history test), and we'd turn on the "Hello, Yew-Awl" radio show that read requests and played hillbilly music for two hours every afternoon. "Wildwood Flower" was our favorite song and we thought that was what they would play in heaven. We also decided that all we'd eat in heaven was chess pie, and that honeysuckle would bloom there all year long.

Sometimes we would play Robin Hood or Indian Princess, which we took from our favorite book, *Green Mansions*. Frances would put on the brightest purple she could find in the lipstick collection—the blue tones, they were called—and she always put it too high and too low so that her mouth seemed to spread all over her face. I preferred the red tones, rose or orange. I would pin rolled-up pairs of socks to the inside of my red and white striped T-shirt for bosoms. We would cinch in our waists to show their smallness with red or blue plastic belts. Sometimes our stomachs got bruised in the process. My waist measured eighteen inches the winter we were ten and eleven, and Frances's sixteen and a half. I applied Indian-dark Leg-Tan to my legs because they were always covered with mosquito bites, except from maybe October to around March, and they never got tanned. The mosquitoes never bit Frances.

She liked fancy upswept hairdos from which floated silk scarves of bright colors. We both wore moccasins from the dime store that said "Made in Japan." We lived underneath a secret waterfall in a cave with walls of gold, and spoke a private language. At one point I bought, also at the dime store, a peach-colored satin plunging bra with flesh-colored lace on it, which was too pretty to wear *underneath* things, so sometimes I just wore it alone, and other times I wore it on top of my shirt, but I always put the socks inside to give it shape.

Frances had gone with me to buy it, but not until I had promised to help her steal a beautiful scarf she wanted. We had decided we could steal only those things we didn't have enough money to buy, things small enough to be hidden (if necessary, forever), and things valuable enough to be worth stealing. In four years we stole only five things. Four really, because the lipsticks couldn't actually be considered stealing since they were all second-hand. We stole: 1) Frances's scarf, turquoise blue and green flowered. 2) A Sparkle Plenty doll for Frances (I had won one on the "Kiddi Karnival Quiz Show" by answering the question, "If you take a piece of material and pink and blue it, what color will it be?" A teen-aged girl missed it by saying "Purple" and I got my chance. I had seen Rose and Dorothy sewing in wartime and knew the answer was "White"). 3) A geranium-pink bathing suit with a "floating bra" that expanded to life-size when you got in the water, which we told Rose I had bought for a dollar at the dime store. (The actual price was $4.98 but Rose must have been fooled because she never batted an eye. I also told her it wasn't for beauty, but safety, that I bought it. It kept you afloat. She only said, "I bet.") And 4) A bicycle, which we took back to Karen Cobb's porch an hour and a half later because it didn't fit our second requirement. How to explain about it? (Besides, we had the impression that Christmas, then only two months away, might bring us both bicycles, which it did.) We knew Karen Cobb and her family had gone to Richmond for the day and had thought far enough ahead to be prepared to paint the red bike black and gold all over to disguise it. We realized we couldn't explain a black and gold bike any more than a red one after we'd finished the paint job. Karen Cobb, who was pretty stupid, never did figure out what had happened. A week later, she painted it red again, though it was much more beautiful gold and black.

But we weren't real thieves. Most things we bought, like the satin bra.

"For you?" the salesgirl had asked.

"Oh, no, it's—for my grandmother."

Silence.

"She's very little," I said. My mouth felt dry. "Just about my size."

"A very little old lady," Frances explained.

But right now there was something sinister and scary in the way Frances was applying the lipstick. She seemed very serious as she outlined her mouth with great care. There was none of the wild fun of our games. And she stayed in the lines. Her odd behavior bothered me so that I couldn't concentrate.

That very afternoon I tried to get her to play our old games, pointing out that the day was pretty boring anyway. Somehow, I thought that if we could just play again, all would be right.

We had never gotten the game of Robin Hood under way without having terrible arguments about who was going to be whom. Frances always wanted to be Maid Marian, which I didn't think was fair because the only other person I could be was Will Scarlett's girlfriend, Jefferson. In the story Will Scarlett was terribly fickle. We tried everyone, but Alan a Dale was too sissy, Little John was too stupid, Friar Tuck couldn't get married and besides was too fat, so we always had to go back to Will Scarlett, despite his bad morals. There was nothing in the rules that said we had to follow the plot, and so we finally fixed the story up and gave Will a sweetheart named Jefferson. But though Will was of all the band second only to Robin Hood himself, he couldn't replace Robin Hood, so we usually had a fight to determine who would get to be Maid Marian for the day.

Today didn't seem like the right day for Robin Hood so I suggested Indian Princess instead. Indian Princess was set in the Wild West instead of in Merry Olde England. We had a treasure chest that contained a small orange Mexican fire opal, which my father had once bought, but never had set, for my mother; a quail's wishbone; the tiniest feather I had ever found; several plastic rings; an arrowhead; and two hollow bullets ordered from cereal boxes, one of which glowed purple-blue in the dark and smelled a little like hard-boiled eggs. Frances was White Feather in this game, and I, Red Flower.

The truth was that most of our games consisted of getting ready to play. Playing Indian Princess really meant exploring the woods near Frances's house and mapping and naming every path and landmark. We were mad for the naming of things and very good at it. We thought up the stories but never got around to acting them out. It wasn't much fun after you'd already made it up because you already knew how it would end.

Today, in the white afternoon, we were in the meadow just behind the house, Frances having agreed to have a go at Indian Princess, though I could see her heart was not in it. We were standing in a hushed field full of Queen Anne's lace and yarrow. No birds sang, and the air was pungent with wild carrot and sharp mint.

"You know," Frances said, chewing a long piece of sheep grass, "you really ought to be Will Scarlett's permanent girl-friend in Robin Hood, because the names are so close: *Red Flower* and Will *Scarlett*." I felt trapped by my own color preference, but could not think of a way to answer. Frances suddenly seemed so cool, so safe, so much *older*, green as tree shade. Everything worked out for her. She stood just before me, casting no shadow, utterly still in the white heat. I sweated and picked a mosquito bite on my elbow; sweat dropped into one eye, making it sting, and causing me to squint even more than usual. Frances never squinted at all.

"They don't have anything to do with each other," I said. I felt the heat like a dead cat around my neck, and knew then we would not play our game today, or perhaps ever again. Maybe when Toby Bright came, he would play with me. Maybe he wouldn't be so bad, after all.

"We could go to the playroom," she said. The day was diamond-hard.

But I got a better idea. "Let's write a note and put it in a bottle and throw it in the river." You could always see the light actually grow in Frances's eyes when something struck her as a really good idea.

"A love note!"

"We can sign it somebody famous, like President Truman. Harry S. Truman."

Scorn. "If it was a love note, it would be signed just 'Harry,' and then whoever found it wouldn't know which Harry it was from."

"But I can copy his handwriting. I've seen it lots of times."

I had been a very good forger since I'd learned to write at the age of five. I had always known what letters were, but then suddenly I could sound out the letters together and hear the word I had just sounded, usually some word I had known for a long time. I learned the silent *k* with the sounded *n* following; learned that *ph* sounds like *f*. Soon I discovered that by putting together the sounds I could write the letters into words. All this I did by myself.

I lived with my aunt then, and one day I took a piece of paper to her in great excitement. After a second or two Dorothy had frowned and asked, "What's this?" I was really destroyed. She never even tried to understand.

"My name," I urged her to see. "Jessie Preston."

"G-E-S-E-P-R-E-S-T-N," she spelled. Then she said, "Not exactly."

"Then show me how," I said.

I practiced it for four days in just letters, then asked her to write it for me like grown-ups, and in a week I could write for real. In copying writing, I discovered my talent as a forger. On walls I wrote Mussolini's name, just as I had seen it written in *Life* magazine's picture of billboards in Italy. To shopping lists in people's kitchens I added "beer" and "light bulbs" and "Flit," careful always to copy exactly the handwriting already on the paper.

The market list game stopped abruptly when I wrote "wiskey" on Dorothy's list. She looked at it in great puzzlement. It was in her handwriting exactly. I stared blankly, enjoying the joke, laughter filling my stomach like a crumpled brown paper bag slowly opening. But Dorothy figured it out and was not amused. She said "Shame" and "Sin" and "Irresponsible" and (looking sideways) "Not even the way to *spell* it." So the game was over, but I never forgot the day when she came from the store bringing Duz, ginger ale, and catsup that she didn't need, and in her mild puzzlement mumbling, "Now let me see, why did I . . . ? We have plenty of catsup . . . don't remember. . . ." It had been hugely amusing, and I was warm with secret success.

Once a couple of years later I wrote Frances a scorching love note and signed it "Phillips Hepwaite." He was a red-haired boy in our class at school with big teeth and a wide grin. The forgery was perfect, and Frances acted very odd. She seemed sometimes to be confident, other times fearful, sometimes full of energy, other times wanting only to sit or loll for days. And the days of summer denumbered. At the end of August she said she could not face him when fifth grade started in a few days, that she hated him, and I told her the truth. Her face fell; she would not speak to me for almost a week. I didn't understand her anger at such a good joke. She had thought it hilarious that very summer when we wrote a note to Karen Cobb saying, "We hate you. We are going to kill you at midnight. The Phantom." But I apologized sincerely, as I was anxious to be in her good graces again, and I told her truthfully I only meant to be funny.

Now I had to keep up the game, to keep everything normal.

"But if he's the president he'd sign it 'Harry T.' at least, wouldn't he?"

"Of *course* not," she said. "And besides, he wouldn't put it in the bottle in the first place. He has a franking privilege. That's . . ."

"I *know* what it is."

"We have to think of something else." Her eyes were dull again. I had to think fast.

"If we could make it look like it came from a long way off . . ."

"Yes! Exactly!" She leapt to her feet. "Listen! We'll sign it 'From Hawaii' or something. Then they'll think it came all that way!"

"How about Alaska? It could get here more logically from Alaska. It's *up.*"

She wrinkled her forehead in a very patient, grown-up way.

"Jessie, if you had the *least* idea of geography—" (That was mean of her. She knew geography was my worst course. I could never remember if they grew rice in China or Holland or if Rome was farther south than Naples), "you'd remember that the Japanese current carries bottles and things over here from Japan *and* Hawaii all the time." (Better to let her win than ruin the game.)

"Well, okay. But how would it get inland?"

"It would work its way upstream, like salmon. It happens all the time in books."

"Then where'll it be from?"

"Hmmm. Maybe Japan." (Joy: I could get even.)

"But how are we going to write Japanese?" I had her there, though I faked wide-eyed innocence.

"Then Maine. That's more logical anyway."

So it was decided. We found a bottle with a top that had lodged in a tree root by the creek. It was half-full of brownish water and still had the label on: "Mineral Oil, U.S.P." We both felt it ought to be a wine or whiskey bottle, but none could be found. I wrote a mysterious note in a flamboyant backhand that read:

23

Whereto a bloody stream doth flow?
Into the life of man!
Where ghostly spirits fond and true,
Are ruled by a ghostly hand.
                    The Phantom
                    Maine, U.S.A.

We scratched out the "ghostly" in the last line and replaced it with "bloody." Frances drew scrolls and roses all
around the edge, and finally we sent the bottle off down-
stream, bobbing and ramming gently into rocks and branches
until it was out of sight. I regretted privately that there was
no way the authors could become known, since it was the sort
of thing that would probably get into the papers. Perhaps
when it did I might step modestly forward as author of the
joke. . . . But we never saw it in the papers, and after a
while I forgot to look.

2

Toby Bright arrived from the bus with Charlie early one morning. Charlie always got up very early and cooked bacon for everyone before he went to work. He was there at breakfast when I came downstairs, my bare feet still dirty from yesterday and the day before, since I only took baths when Rose told me to. I hadn't known he would be there. Rose had told us "morning" but I was taken by surprise.

He was about as tall as I was, but much thinner, and he was the ugliest boy I had ever seen. I tried to pretend not to see him, sneaking my information in tiny glances as I let my gaze wander around the room, bounce off the ceiling, study the brown floor, outline the disapproving portrait of Frances's great-grandfather. Toby Bright was very neatly dressed, I noted, in brown pants like Charlie wore instead of blue jeans, a light blue shirt, and very brightly polished brown shoes. I kept gazing around, practicing my new trick—touching the end of my nose with the tip of my tongue. His hair was beige and frizzly; he had grayish skin with terrible scars all over his face and neck, more even than I had on my legs. Besides that, he was slightly cross-eyed and had very thick glasses that made his eyes seem very little and far away. The sunshine streamed into the dining room just behind him, causing a brightness of yellow around his fuzzy head. He was fourteen, nearly fifteen, I already knew, two years ahead of me, one and a half grades ahead of Frances.

I was still gazing around the room, glued to the newel post and the last step of that stupid stairway that came into the dining room instead of (as in proper houses) the hall. I would have to notice in a minute that he was there. Just as I was trying to figure out what to say, Frances came down the stairs behind me, and I noticed that she was walking in a peculiar way that I couldn't figure out, but could hear. I turned around to see, and it had something to do with taking littler steps, much littler than usual. I noted too that her bottom was always in motion. I was reminded of Maid Marian's walk, not unlike, but more exaggerated than, this new one. I wished very much that Rose were there. I could think of nothing to say to Toby Bright so I asked Frances why she was walking so funny. I was absolutely unprepared for the freezing scorn it caused, her angry sweeping exit upward from the breakfast scene, leaving Toby Bright and me alone again. I could hear her running upstairs at her usual pace and her door shutting with a bright red bang. I stared at my feet and the dark boards of the floor beneath, as if something to say might be written there.

"Guess Frances doesn't want any breakfast," I said.

"She ate before I came. She didn't think you were up yet."

"Well, I am," I said cleverly, then it didn't sound clever.

"You're Jessie. I'm Toby Bright." He made these two statements very slowly, quite solemnly.

"I know." I scratched my head. No miracle occurred. No handwriting appeared on the floor. Light bulb. "What's for breakfast?"

"Grits," he said.

So I went to the kitchen (in gigantic relief) to get some, wondering where Rose was, why Frances got so mad, what I had done. After I had taken as much time as I could, and could think of no reason to stay in the kitchen any longer, I took my grits and bacon to the table, remembered milk, returned for it, and sat down in my place, which happened to be directly across the table from Toby Bright. He looked frankly at me, and I snuck a look at him, taking huge exaggerated bites so he would know I was not paying any attention to him. When the silence grew unbearable, I sighed deeply and scratched at a new mosquito bite on the back of my hand, trying to calm the panic I felt. I was actually startled when he spoke.

"Do you have a bike?"

"Sure," I said loudly, mouth full of grits. "Do you?"

He nodded.

"I can ride no hands."

"Oh." He said it just like he had said, "You're Jessie." Then, shaking his head slowly from one side to the other and making a clicking noise with his mouth, "Your feet sure do look tough."

"Oh, they *are*," I said, complimented. "I can walk on anything. Think I'll carve my initials in my heels." I forced a yawn to prove that I was not really interested in this conversation. "I read in a book once where a boy did that."

"Wow," he said. "What book?"

"Some Hardy Boys mystery, I think. I forget which one." I ate a whole piece of bacon in one bite, leaning my head back to get it all in without breaking it. I was nearly to the best part of the grits, the center, the buttery part. I had eaten them from the outside in, around and around, always getting nearer the center, snail-shape.

"I like to read those too," he said, "but I don't remember *that*."

"Well, it's there," I said. "Frances doesn't like the Hardy Boys."

He didn't say anything to that, so I sat back, swallowed my vitamin pill slickly, rolled my eyes, and cast about for something else to say, rubbing my stomach. He just looked at me, unsmiling, out of those tiny eyes. I was afraid he'd missed the pill part, as he didn't comment.

"Well, guess I'll take my vitamin pill."

"You've already taken it. Just a minute ago."

"Oh, did I?" He simply nodded. "Mostly I just take it right down by itself, but once I took it with beer. I don't remember how I took it just now." A careless laugh.

"That's how you took it."

"With beer?"

"No, by itself."

"Oh," I nodded. He had indeed noticed.

"Well," I said finally.

"What?"

"Yessir, they're tough okay." I hoisted one foot up and scratched between my toes. He smiled, and looked even sillier than he did without the smile.

"You can say that again," he said.

"What?"

"I said, 'You can say that again.' "

"Oh," I said.

He smiled again, bit his lip, took his napkin out of his lap, and carefully placed it beside his plate.

"Ha, ha. Yessir, they're tough okay."

Silence.

"Don't you get it?" I asked, leaning across the table. "You said, 'You can say that again,' and I *said* it again. Don't you get it?"

"Oh!" he said. "Yeah! Sure I do!"

"Jessie!" yelled Frances, from the top of the steps. I did not hear her coming, and wondered if she had been listening. "Come quick! Quick!"

"Unh—excuse me, I gotta go," I said.

"Glad to meet you."

"Same here." On my way out of the dining room, I ran smack into the china closet with my hipbone. The huge ugly thing shuddered dangerously and I fled, my side zinging with pain that crazed out in all directions from the center of the blow.

"What do you want?"

"Oh—nothing."

"*Nothing!* You said 'quick!' "

"Well—I just noticed you didn't make up your bed." She was certainly right about that. I hadn't made up my bed since Dorothy died.

"My bed! What in the heck are you talking about? We *never* make our beds!" But hers was indeed neatly made up. In fact, her whole room had undergone some strange transformation. "Where are the dolls?" I asked.

She shrugged. "Oh, they were cluttering things up so I just put them away."

"Oh. Hey, about your walking—" But she turned on me.

"Never mind! Just why do you have to *ask* me about everything?"

"You just looked funny, that's why. The way your fanny—"

"SHUT UP!"

"I will not. I'm going downstairs and talk to Toby Bright." She looked as if she had smelled something bad. I sensed the truth. "He's only here for two days," I said, "and I don't see that it can hurt to be nice to him. He's a Very Nice Boy." She glared daggers at me. "Why don't you like him?"

"I TOLD you to stop asking everything!" And she slammed shut her closet door with all the might in her arm.

"Well, toodle-oo; I'm going to talk to him," I said gaily. "I don't think he's so bad. 'Bye!"

I would have been perfectly willing to lie on this point to please or annoy Frances, to be with her or against her at my convenience. At that moment I was irritated with her and feeling off balance about her room, so I defended Toby Bright. Secretly, I thought he was the goofiest boy I had ever seen, though certainly one of the nicest, his compliment still causing a warmth to creep up my neck. I could have concentrated my efforts on either trait, the goofiness or the niceness, and continued to feel that way. The real reason I decided to like Toby Bright was that Frances did not and I was not in a mood to agree with her. I remembered that my Aunt Dorothy had usually decided likings and dislikings that way.

It's funny that Dorothy's image appeared before me at that moment. She popped into my head as though she were alive and standing before me. Her hands and eyes were always cold, and her mouth shiny with cold cream because her lips were dry and cracked so much of the time. She smelled of starch and violet bath salts. When I lived with her I had tried my best to stay away from her except at mealtimes, because I gave her headaches. She never liked the people I liked, and all the time said that the neighborhood had been much nicer when my mother was little, before I was born, before there was a cemetery, when all you could see in every direction was fields and sky. For instance, I liked Mrs. Miller who one day in the summertime taught me how to make vinegar taffy, and while we made it we sang hymns—not the ones we sang in church, but the kind we heard on "Hello, Yew-All." At supper Dorothy had said that Mrs. Miller was common, that the taffy had ruined my appetite, and that I was not to go back there again.

I didn't want to decide things the way Dorothy did, but it honestly seemed to me there was no reason to dislike Toby Bright, especially since Frances didn't like him.

Downstairs, I could tell that Rose was washing clothes from the rhythmic *sludge, sludge, sludge, sludge* sounds on the porch. Toby Bright was reading the paper, holding it up very close to his face. I had never seen a kid read like that before. Besides, none of the people I knew my age read newspapers, except for the comic page, or, like me, when my picture was in it. Toby Bright was reading the actual articles. He put it down and smiled his foolish smile when I came in. This time I had memorized what I would say.

"Do you want to go on a bike ride?" I recited. "You can ride Frances's."

"Okay," he said solemnly, nodding slowly. Frances was upstairs, Rose was busy, so we just went. We got the bikes and walked them down the crunching driveway to the curve leading out to the road.

Neither of us talked. Bouncing along the narrow road I

called back over my shoulder, "We can ride out to the air-port!"

He smiled and nodded without answering.

I was done in by the perfectly glorious day. My feelings were softened toward Toby Bright, and even Frances, as we rode through layers and layers of creamy sunshine, warm, kind, so that when you raised your face with your eyes crinkled closed, your hair swept back, you still saw light, orange-red, through your lids.

I leaned back into the pillowy air as though it would support me. The road rose and fell drunkenly. We labored uphill and loafed coasting down, swooping upward again from the cool shadowy hollows.

The smells of honeysuckle and wild roses and tar, the cool wind sound and the droning of bees, the waterfall sunshine in cascades, lay heavy upon this day, upon all the world, it seemed, and a small blacksnake barely wiggled across the road in time for me to miss it. I cried to Toby Bright and pointed. He had not seen the snake, and we stopped and looked for it in the high weeds, sweeter-smelling and cleaner than any soap or perfume. When we couldn't find it, we rode on without talking much. The world was wetly green, like when I looked at its wavy image through the giant water bottle on the side porch. Toby Bright was as good a rider as I was, even though he looked puny.

At a long narrow meadow we stopped and fed some grass to a red horse, and Toby Bright showed me a field sparrow's nest. It still had some little bits of shell in it. I asked him how he knew what kind of bird lived in it, and he smiled a tiny mysterious smile and said, as though it were the most natural thing in the world, that it was different from all the other kinds of nests. It looked just like any other nest to me.

I asked him if he could show me a field sparrow and he said, "They're all gone now. But we might see one later. Sometime we will." The promise was rich and I remembered it. He took the nest, picking it up slowly with great care. He said the birds wouldn't use it anymore. Before we left, we went back to rub the fuzzy soft nose of the horse.

"Do you think horses in Europe neigh in European?" he asked slowly, his hand resting on the brick-red velvet nose.

"I never thought about it," I admitted. "But they wouldn't know how to in English, would they?"

"I wonder if they sound different."

"We'd have to go there to find out, I guess."

"We'll do that someday. You know, they have different kinds of birds and insects in Europe than here. I'd love to see them all."

Suddenly I knew that I would too. I wanted to so much it took away my breath, so much I could not even say it. So, instead, walking back to the bikes, I said, "I wonder if they can ever make a perfume that smells like this day." Toby Bright didn't answer and I wasn't even sure he had heard. He was looking at something in his hand.

"What?" I asked. He held it out. It was a beetle with a hard burnished shell, or maybe I could see only a speck of the shell—bronze, burgundy, apple, blue, all of a single color, a single silence, the entire summer upon that tiny back. All things seemed to turn on that one thing. Then the beetle moved a leg. Toby Bright looked at me and smiled.

"Are all bugs that pretty up close?" I asked. Then immediately I felt silly because it sounded dumb.

"I think so," he said, and I saw that he didn't think it was a stupid question.

At the airport we stopped and walked around. It had been

a wartime airport and hadn't been used for three years. The runway was overgrown with weeds now, and we traced it to the very end. Then I showed Toby Bright the bubbling spring. It was the best spring I knew, clear and cold, full even in the hottest driest weather, its water slowed by a matty jungle of watercress. A huge turtle plopped into the water from a log as we came near. Toby Bright had never eaten watercress. He sampled it, slow and thoughtful, finally smiling. I was very pleased to show him something new, and we ate together, squatting near the edge of the spring, our feet aching in the cold water. I had never put shoes on; he had taken off his and left them very neatly at the water's edge, each white sock carefully stuffed into its proper shoe. His eyes were very kind in back of his glasses, though it was sometimes hard to tell where he was looking.

We picked some watercress to take home for lunch, and I picked some butter-and-eggs and chicory to give to him. I discovered with a flush of heat that I couldn't present him with the flowers because they meant so much all of a sudden. So I said they were for Rose. We didn't have any way to carry the watercress home. Any other day I would have taken off my shirt to wrap it in. Today I thought of that and felt my neck grow hot, so I did not suggest it. I started to ask Toby Bright to lend his shirt, but two things stopped me. His shirt was still perfectly clean and crisp (my own was sweaty and rumpled)—it would be a pity to ruin it. And I thought about the scars which I almost knew were on his back. I reckoned he might not want anyone to see them, though I would not have minded. He picked a long-stemmed Queen Anne's lace and we wrapped the stem around the bunch of watercress and he carried it home on the handlebars of Frances's bike, along with the sparrow nest. I carried Toby Bright's flowers home to Rose, sticky in my fist.

The airport was in an open field, and returning to the road I again was joyfully aware of the honeysuckle that grew all along either side of it. I felt drunk with possession. Never before had *our* country, *our* summer, *our* things, been so lovely as seen by me through new eyes, through the clouded magnified gaze of Toby Bright. I shouted out the names Frances and I had given to every landmark: Nottingham Road, Key Island, Apache Cove! I breathed in deeply and wished for this day to stay. I wanted the smell of honeysuckle to be a forever thing.

I was filled with happiness and energy. I rode no hands, praying that Toby Bright would see. Sitting straight up, eyes slitted against the breeze I myself created, I pedaled vigorously uphill and tore down so fast it frightened me. We were coming down the last hill that led directly into the driveway when I turned to see if Toby Bright was watching me.

His warning noise, not a yell, more like a bark—just a noise —came too late. My bike went into a skid, the gravel rattled like a machine gun, and I was pitched onto the roadside just at our driveway entrance. My eyes were blinded by dust and spurting tears; my right side had grated along the rocks for many feet. I lay with my cheek unbearably scratched on the sharp gravel, but I did not try to move it. I pushed it into the gravel more until the pain was maroon, darker than red, darker, black. Toby Bright's flowers lay like bright gems along the ground, blue and golden.

Stupid, clumsy, dumb, show-off rang around the rosy in the ringing bloody darkness of my brain. In the area of my nose and forehead bright lights flashed on and off. I tried to struggle to my feet. Toby Bright was off his bike, running, from the sound of his feet, *pat, p-tat, pat, p-tat,* coming close, stooping, trying to help me up, only I was bigger than he was.

"Are you okay?" he said. I reached up to push my hair out of my face and wept with anger and pain. I struggled to my poor bloody knees, trying at the same time to pick up the bike, and he helped me.

"I'm okay," I wheezed, bubbling tears and spit, angry, teeth gritty-clenched. "So give me the bike, I'm okay." But he wouldn't let me alone, and seemed incredibly cool and clean and soap-scented in his blue shirt. My vision of him jerked a little before my muddy eyes as he tried to pat me.

"Please don't cry, Jessie." He was frowning. I could not stop crying and knew exactly how I must look to him, my face grimy and disheveled, all the confidence and glory of the instant before gone, broken. I hid my face in my hands and cried harder. He moved nearer and I could hear his breathing and smell a sort of faint grassy smell.

"Jessie, please." His voice was even closer, coming on a wisp of warm breath against my hands. "Are you hurt?" I shook my head, still protecting my face. Suddenly his hands were very carefully taking my hands away. Shapes swam in front of my eyes and my face felt red and hot. Into the watery glass of my vision swam the ugly moon-surfaced face of Toby Bright. His eyes crossed extremely behind the heavy glasses, and for just an instant time seemed to stand still. I was a bug under a microscope, and in all the world there were just we two. I could smell the sunshine on the skin of Toby Bright, and see around his head the same halo of light as that morning.

"Sorry," he was murmuring very softly, *pat, pat*, "wish you wouldn't cry. Are you hurt? Sorry. Please don't, Jessie. Jessie." I wished I had been killed instead of this. I shook my head, answering, and felt my face twist up red-monkey-like to begin to cry again. I saw myself dirty, clumsy, shamed, and my misery increased. His hand was still absently patting my shoulder, my back, the back of my head, my arm. Over and over he said, "Don't cry, please don't cry." Quite abruptly, his face came closer; his nose bumped mine. His eyes absurdly, comically crossed, he kissed me, his lips dry and soft as a raspberry. I stopped crying and kept my eyes closed, but it didn't happen again. There was a quick leap inside me somewhere, an ache in the loins, a sweet liquid surge.

In an instant, I pushed him away, suddenly aware of kissing. Broad daylight; Frances, Rose, the driveway! World! Sin! —*What if someone saw?* I jerked the bike up and began to wheel it blindly toward the house, and I couldn't know whether the wreck or Toby Bright's kiss had shaken me more. I could not look at him or speak to him, and his voice reached me thin on the air as I was going into the house.

"Jessie." Half a question, half a statement. But I went on. I managed to avoid seeing anyone, went directly to the bathroom, locked the door, brushed my teeth several times, washing my mouth very hard. I tried to clean up the scratches, giving up when it hurt, turning my attention to my chewing gum, which had got full of gravel and dirt. After some minutes I realized there was not even a small part of it I could save and so I gave up and watched with regret as my key to fame went spiraling down the toilet.

My wounds were gruesome, as I stared at myself swollen and scratched in the bathroom mirror. I called down to summon Rose and when she arrived *poof*ing at the top of the stairs, I announced that I did not want any lunch. Everyone else had eaten in our absence, and having to face Toby Bright in my humility alone across a lunch table was impossible. For good measure, I said I also would not be present for supper and wished to go to bed. She expressed light concern over my

skinned parts, offering Mercurochrome, but did not understand my wanting to go to bed. I explained that I didn't feel
well, and it came into my head to say that maybe I was get-
ing the curse. I knew all about that, from a book Rose had
given Frances and me. She asked if I were bleeding and I told
her, modestly, just a little. It was not a lie. My arm and cheek
were still oozing tiny globs of blood. *I cannot look at Toby
Bright again.* Rose provided me with an elastic belt, a pad,
and a bottle of hydrogen peroxide for my wounds, and went
away. It still hurt to work on the wounds, but somewhere I
had heard that a dog licking its wounds caused them to heal
faster, so I tried that for a while, licking until my tongue was
numb and dry and my mouth crumbly all over again. So I
brushed my teeth once more until the gums bled. Finally I got
into bed, gingerly arranging my body which to me felt broken
and bleeding, trying not to move, and filled with anxiety.

I was reasonably sure no one saw; I was crazy to know
what they would talk about downstairs; restlessly I tossed
off the covers but very quickly pulled them up again. Toby
Bright might come up to see me.

At the thought, I sat stark upright in bed, then leapt out
to peer anxiously at my face in the mirror. After listening
carefully at the door, I dashed on tiptoe into the bathroom,
worked on my face and arms some more, and combed my hair
carefully. I added just a hint of Rose's lipstick, rubbing it in
thoroughly.

I hurried back to my room, carefully smoothed up the bed
and puffed the pillow, and arranged three Hardy Boys books
carelessly on the bedcover. Then, remembering that I was an
invalid, I lay down and turned the worst side of my face toward the pillow.

I woke up and read by the light outside that it was nearly suppertime. I lay still and hungry, wondering what to do. I could not read: I had read those three before and I dared not get up again; I was very hungry. I closed my eyes tight as coffins, wishing I had some blue eye shadow for my sunken lids, wondering if crayon would do, and waited, dying to go to the bathroom. My heart bounded at footsteps on the stairs. It was probably Toby Bright because they didn't sound like Rose's or Frances's or Charlie's. I held my breath when the door opened, and tried to look beautifully frail and near death. In the last instant I remembered to let my tongue loll out and in the same instant was sorry to have forgotten to cross my hands on my chest.

It was only Frances, precariously carrying my supper on a tray. She was wearing her new high-heel shoes. No wonder she had not sounded right. She was stinking of perfume and dressed in her best red dress.

"You going somewhere?" I asked, in what I hoped was a faint voice, not moving in case there was someone else with her. There wasn't, and she didn't notice my near-death state.

"Just dinner, silly." I closed my eyes, hating her, hating especially the sophisticated perfume that filled the room, pushing out the memory of honeysuckle. "Toby told us about the wreck. Are you all right? You look all right to me." I waited in terror, but she was through. "He's really stupid," she said as she left.

I lay in bed, listening to the rise and fall of voices below, touching my lips with my fingers to see what they had felt like to Toby Bright. Frances was down there with them, and I reckoned that she had somewhat changed her mind about Toby Bright, as occasionally I heard her laugh. Mostly, though, the sounds were of Rose and Toby Bright talking, no words distinguishable, and every now and then Charlie's voice, slow, brief. After an hour or so I felt I had to go out somewhere, into the night; that I was not at all sleepy, and could not bear to stay in bed. I knew I looked awful, all blue and hamburgery and tweedy. I would not have minded my looks at all if I had only been attacked by a circus lion or run over by a truck. I was also afraid to face Toby Bright. I would have to go by the open door of the living room to get to either the front or back door.

Eventually I could stay in bed no longer. I got up and put on my blue jeans and a big gray sweater of Frances's and sneaked downstairs through the dining room, taking each step carefully just in the middle, feeling my way like an Indian. Light coming from the living room door lay in a wide yellow band across the hall. By the door, I was stopped short in the dark by the sound of my own name.

"Jessie's okay, isn't she?" Toby Bright was asking, in his solemn way. "She seemed okay."

I held my breath and prayed: Do not tell them. Do not. You wouldn't. You wouldn't. In a moment, as I listened, I knew: He wouldn't. I leaned against a door, dizzy from the strain. I relaxed, then recalled I had run all the way into the house after the accident. It would have been much better to crawl. The newspaper headlines appeared before my eyes: WOUNDED GIRL CRAWLS HOME TO DIE; I very nearly choked on the throat lump that started up at the thought. Then I hesitated in the dark. What if they discovered me? I just had to go out. Down on my stomach, I began to wiggle wormlike across the band of light.

"Oh, there she is now! Jessie, what are you doing? Come on in. Join us. Feeling better?" And Rose asked this last with embarrassing significance. My sore nose was pushed down into the rug as far as I could get it. Stiffly I struggled to my knees, and finally, with the help of the doorjamb, made it to my feet. I edged into the doorway, my eyes upon the bony, huge, dirt-and-blood-streaked feet. In my washing, as usual, I had not gotten that far south. As I was staring at them, I tripped and slammed to my knees in front of them all. I heard Frances give a delicate little gasp.

"Still barefoot," Toby Bright said solemnly, half a statement, half a question. Frances, feet Sunday-shod, sat with her lips pressed together and her ankles crossed. The lions' den would be heaven compared to this. I was furious with Toby Bright for mentioning my bare feet, though there was no mockery in his voice. I had never seen Frances sit like that before.

"I have never seen you sit that way before," I said loudly and angrily to Frances. "Why are you sitting that *funny* way?" She looked as though she had just sucked half a lemon. Toby Bright was leaning toward me, staring at me through his glasses.

"Are you okay?" When I didn't answer, he continued, "I didn't think you were hurt very much, maybe just scared. You're all right now?" That same funny half question.

Not hurt. I will die and you will all be sorry. All of you. Lying in a little white coffin covered with white roses. No. Pink ones. The black headlines: GONE BUT NOT FORGOTTEN.

"Jessie." That was Charlie's voice and when he spoke it was the color of maple syrup and everyone listened. I looked up. "Come in and sit down here." Charlie patted the seat beside him. I could only shake my head. "Then what are you going to do?" he asked mildly. He had gone way over his quota of words-at-one-time.

"Going out," I managed to croak.

"Better put some shoes on," he commented. I did not reply, but tried to hide my disreputable feet beneath each other, toes crimped under. It only served to streak and dirty them more.

"Yes," Frances agreed, "it must be very uncomfortable to go barefoot all the time." That was the fakiest thing I had ever heard, especially the way she sneered on "barefoot." I remained silent, unable to think of anything scathing enough to utter.

"She's shy," Frances explained clearly, leaning chummily toward Toby Bright. *I threw a dagger directly at her heart. She turned into a toad. Nobody noticed.*

I saw that Toby Bright did not notice her comment, or did not seem to. Still I hated her. *Common*, the worst name I knew, worse even than *pussy*, leapt to my lips and I bit it off just in time, killing it. I saw that my fingers, laced together, were white at the knuckles, though pale blue grew along the outside of the right one.

"Maybe we can go for another ride tomorrow," Toby Bright said. I kept on looking at the rug braided like my hair was when I was younger. I shook my head again.

"I—can't. I hafta do my—homework," I whispered.

"Homework!" yelled Frances. "*Homework* in the *summer!*" she howled.

I hated her, hated her, fat toad, ugly green dressed-up toad. *A toad with prim crossed ankles. She begs for her life. I go off and leave her and pretty soon somebody steps on her.*

"Frances!" Rose said. "That's enough. Jessie, you look hot. Go get something to drink. You and Toby can decide later." She brought the brown sweater she was knitting up close to her face and began to count something on it. I fled.

A milkshake would make me feel better. I was in the green

slick kitchen pouring milk into a tall jelly glass with red tulips on it, the linoleum cool as clay under my feet, when I heard a footstep. I whirled around to face Toby Bright. Too late, I remembered the milk bottle in my hand. It slipped, spinning onto the floor, did not break, but milk foamed out white and blue all over.

"Oh, look; I'll get that," he said, kneeling down to pick up the bottle as though nothing had happened. I could not move from misery. My eyes were tight closed with tears squeezing out from beneath the lids. The iron rim of the sink pushed my backbone through to my stomach. The smell of straw and skin was like a voice from this afternoon. A bit of breeze blown from the road, the gravel, the kiss. A flash of memory: the morels:

"We could ride into town," he was saying, looking up at me. "Would you like to have the nest we found? I gave your flowers to Rose, and the watercress." He was kneeling in front of me with spilled milk all around. I dared not move, breathe, speak, but if I didn't breathe soon I would die. MISS JESSIE PRESTON HOLDS BREATH LONGER THAN ANY LIVING PERSON. The word "we" embarrassed me. I was horrified he might reach his hand the few inches needed to touch me.

Before the summer had started, but the same year, during the most fragrant part of spring, Frances and I had hunted the morels. We knew what they were because we had read about them in an English novel. This man had wanted to kill his wife so he had brought home two kinds of mushrooms, the pretty but deadly Destroying Angel, pure white, and the repugnant-looking morel, counting upon her selfishness to assure that he got the ugly one, she the gorgeous white one. She fixed them both in cream sauces, and conscience-smitten for the first time in all those years, gave him the pretty white one. Anyhow, we knew what a lot of things like that were like, and spent a lot of time hunting snipes, truffles, and morels until some friend of Rose's pointed out to us that an ocean separated us from all those things. Slope-eyed, we gave up, and after that looked only for berries we knew, and greens, and nuts. Frances and I loved exotic foods, especially artichokes, avocadoes, and the field mushrooms which we had always picked in the fall with Charlie. We greeted the wild things like old friends, and knew the dates of every plant and berry and edible weed around.

Morels, sadly, do not exist in our side of the ocean. Except that one day in the woods Frances spotted one. We could not believe our eyes, but it was so different from anything else it had to be a morel. It emerged, a rubbery-looking brown sponge, from the crumbling base of a burnt-out stump. I especially knew the dangers of eating unidentified wild things, having once eaten poison ivy taking it for sassafras, but we picked it anyway, fingering its damp cold flesh more animal-like than vegetable. That had been early in the afternoon in wet rotting woods near the creek, the ground spongy under-foot and icy on our newly bare feet still blue-white from winter, the sun above thin but warm on our heads. We searched until our backs ached from bending aside the springy laurels and rhododendrons, the mayapple umbrellas, the tril-lium leaves. Time and time again there was nothing, yet we persisted. By sundown we had seven of them, miraculous, and we bore them home. It was like finding buried treasure. I was in love with their color, their scent, their shapes—like Christ-mas trees, like lungs, like sponges, springing erect out of the mysterious body of earth.

Rose said they were indeed morels, and that we might cook

them. She suggested we fry them in butter. So we brushed off the dirt with loving care, and melted some butter. My whole body yearned for them. Carefully we laid them in the butter after savoring for the last time their raw fragrance, memory of earth and roots and spring and moistness, swallowing the spurting saliva, glands aching for satisfaction which I knew would surpass all anticipation. We watched them begin their slow collapse, kept our unblinking eyes on them in growing horror as the worms emerged, tiny, writhing, earth-colored, terrible, legion, all falling before our eyes to death in the smoking acrid butter. We both screamed for Rose. I didn't think the destruction of Sodom and Gomorrah any worse than what we witnessed. I cried; Frances just gazed in horror. I learned three things that day: that grown-ups were not always right, what *sauté* meant, and a peculiar aura of nausea that had some connection with love and some connection with death, I did not know what.

This same sensation engulfed me then in the kitchen, as I stood in the presence of Toby Bright and spilled milk.

"Jessie." Toby Bright said, "don't be mad at me." I did not answer, only stared at the foamy milk fanned out on the floor. He reached one hand very slowly toward me, and I shrank back. But he was not reaching for me, only balancing himself. He stood up, holding the empty milk bottle, and put it on the sink edge a few inches from my arm. "Look," he said, reaching for the pink sponge on the edge of the sink, "I'm sorry if you're mad. I'm really sorry. I had a good time today. I'd really like to go riding again." There followed a long terrible pause in which he mopped up the thin-looking milk. A folk song skipped through my brain: *I would I were on yonder hill; 'Tis there I'd sit and cry my fill . . .* ANY-

WHERE, ANY HERE, ANY ELSE. Suddenly I could not stand the silence any longer.

"I bet you think I never . . ." but I could not say the word, . . . "did that before. Well, you're wrong. I did, lots of times. About a million times, I guess." He stopped wiping up the milk and looked at me in his expressionless way, frowning just a little. I could feel heat flare into my neck and face at my boldness. My stomach began to feel the way it did in the afternoon, the way it did on the day of the morels. He stood up, carefully placing the sponge on the sink edge, and fixed his glasses on his nose.

"I've had a lot of wrecks too," he said. "Don't feel bad."

I could make no sense out of what he was talking about, and I couldn't think of anything else to say, so I just stood as I was. After endless time had passed, my whole life like a drowning person's had flickered across my eyes—I had grown old looking at Toby Bright's face, memorizing every fleck in his eyes, every pit of his gray skin—he blinked and spoke.

"Good night." It was very formal, like the end of a movie or a play. Then he smiled a little smile just as he was leaving. "I think going barefoot is much nicer than wearing shoes."

Something like an earthquake occurred in my brain. He had heard. Why, then, none of them mattered. Not Frances. Not Charlie. Not Rose. But I did not allow myself to grin until he had left and the paneled door swung shut on rose-colored air.

I went up the stairs again, tiptoed like a fairy into my room, and closed the door behind me. I was shivering but my face felt burning hot where it was scratched. I had never felt this ice-fire, blue-red, sad-happy way before. I felt skinned. Like a cup filled to overflowing, the tears came, and I cried deeply, face down on my bed, shaking all over. I wished I were six again, or four or five or seven or eight, or even ten, but not this. It seemed that my heart literally ached in my chest with a pain that nothing would relieve. The murmur of voices below me filled me with an anguish that I felt would continue forever and ever, until I died.

It was another night long ago. I got up and went down the steps, skipping fourteen and sixteen because they squeaked. The Ludens were across the street in the bushes, in front of the Strokers' house. I knew Jesus was watching, but I got them anyway.

I stole them today from Mr. Hopkins's drugstore, while I was buying medicine for Dorothy, and put them in the doll carriage under Jane's pillow, while Brown Sugar watched me beady-eyed. Then I wheeled the carriage home and hid them in the box bush.

All through supper I thought of them, and all the evening as it got dark, and all through bedtime. I listened carefully for Dorothy to go to bed.

Now it was silver and cold. In my bare feet I stepped on a slug. Over and over I wiped my foot on the wet grass until it was all gone. I scrabbled around very quietly until I found the cough drops. I started to open them, pulling the red cellophane strip from around one end, then sliding the cellophane off the box. Even the opening of the cardboard box was exciting—to find the half-round place, press it in with a finger, and lift the top.

I carefully tore off the tabs inside the top and threw them away, into the darkness around the roots of the bush. Now I was at the slick waxed paper around them in their neat lovely orange box. My mouth watered, and I began to unfold the paper.

Too much noise.

I crossed the street again, took them back to our porch where it was black in the shadows. Finally they came open, slick and dry long circles on which I could feel the raised letters that spelled Ludens. They crackled very loudly over the crickety, whispering sounds of night.

I ate one. It was sweet and cold, and even the shape was lovely in my mouth. I ate another, two releasing their juices as sweet as honey, but not fast enough. The ache in my jaw was too much. I bore down, and the glassy beads shattered in my mouth. I would not stop now until the whole box was gone.

Getting up the stairs was easier. I hid the cough drops in the hamper, then took them out. It was a favorite hiding place whenever we played hide-and-seek. The bathtub. Underneath, behind the claw feet. No. Each time I changed the hiding place I took one. My bureau drawer. Dorothy might discover them there. My sweaters and blouses. Not safe. Jane's carriage. Not secure, as last week on the street Lady knocked it over with her tail. Brown Sugar stared at me from the carriage, but didn't speak.

Now the Ludens were nearly gone, only a few left. What about the box, the evidence?

I removed the few remaining pieces of candy, and tore the box up into little tiny pieces. I worked up the courage to flush the toilet. It made a tremendous racket. I peered in, and they were all gone. Now I could sleep.

I noticed that the few drops left in my hand were getting sticky, and their smell was no longer nice. One thing about Jesus. No matter what he saw, he never told Dorothy, or anyone else that I knew of. But Jesus still saw. I counted, and there were five left. Finally I hid the cough drops in my Sunday hat, which would not come out again for six days. Unless someone died.

Back in bed, I could not get warm. My feet were icy and my stomach ached. Jesus saw and the stomachache was punishment. As it got worse and worse, I promised Jesus not to eat any more cough drops, and I would prove it:

So I got up and carefully removed the tissue paper from the hat and the cough drops from the tissue paper. I opened the window slowly to keep it from squeaking, and dropped them down through the darkness into the deep bed of day lilies below.

The stomachache persisted.

"Please, Jesus," I said in a whisper, "I will never steal anything again. Or eat candy again." But the savage pain jabbed at my insides.

Dorothy said my mother was pretty because she never ate candy, just apples and things. And that would make you beautiful. Ruefully I thought, I will never be beautiful, I will never eat candy again. In my stomach the gray pain spread, faded, and returned to concentrate into a solid mass.

I struggled awake upward, through layers of time, my insides sore not from candy but from the wreck.

I had dreamed of a time seven years ago, more than one-half my life. In the dark now, I felt my way across the room to the small brown rocking chair we had brought here after Dorothy died, and I found Brown Sugar. Something in his smell, his plushy prickly fur, comforted me, and I stopped shaking. What was it? I kept thinking of Frances, horribly and easily beautiful, sitting downstairs in her red dress, party shoes, smooth dark hair, perfume. Toby Bright! Only my bare feet pleased him. I sat up in the dark, suddenly resolved, suddenly calm, my cheeks crackly from the tears dried on them.

"I know what," I said aloud. "I will go barefoot all summer for you." In the darkness I grinned to myself. I could see the headlines: BORDEN GIRL HOLDS WORLD RECORD, or maybe: BORDEN GIRL WINS ONE MILLION DOLLARS, and Toby Bright and I could live happily ever after. I lay down again on my side with Brown Sugar comfortably in the curve of my body. Soon I heard them all say good night, and the other footsteps on the stairs. Pretty soon Rose's steps came to my door, stopped, and waited. So I pretended to be asleep. She came in and pulled the quilt up over me; it was the only piece of bedclothing I was not lying on. Then she went, closing the door with a click behind her.

Toby Bright and I did not go riding the next day, or ever. Frances was very lively at breakfast, commented sweetly about the improvement in my health, the state of my homework, the ride I was going to take with (I wished she would turn into a bowl of oatmeal and swallow herself) my *boyfriend*. But the word was like knighthood or a spell upon me. A sudden paralysis struck, extending even to my vocal chords as Toby Bright silently appeared at the top of the steps. His shiny white tennis shoes were noiseless as he floated downward into the diffused sunlight of the dining room. Frances, with her back to him, could not hear.

My mouth was full of oatmeal and Frances said, "He really is the stupidest, ugliest, puniest . . ." Her voice rang in the silence, trailed off as if she could not quite figure out . . . her eyes cut around to the right, followed by her head; she caught sight of him, flashed me a look full of fury, and she said clearly, ". . . Dog we ever had. Yessir, that Barney was one dumb dog." And she stretched back luxuriously, giving me a look of triumph. "Morning, Toby," she drawled. He was solemn as ever. Frances came out smelling like a rose.

"I thought you weren't up yet," I croaked.

I bolted for our old playroom over the garage to read in the semidarkness that Rose said would drive me blind if I read in it. But I had read that the eye was a muscle, and I knew that muscles got stronger when they were exercised, so I reasoned that reading in the dark was good for your eyes. It was bound to be true because Frances wore glasses and I didn't, while I read in the dark more than she ever thought of doing. I kept this knowledge secret and planned to patent it when I grew up, and make a million dollars. BORDEN GIRL DISCOVERS MIRACLE CURE, or MISS JESSIE PRESTON HAS BEST EYES IN THE WHOLE WORLD. Downstairs, I heard Frances asking Rose where I was, and Rose's answer that she didn't know.

Lunchtime came: my hunger was stronger even than my embarrassment. Hotter, colder, fuller, emptier, than I had thought possible, I checked my face in the wavy dusty mirror but still could not see who I was. Rose had often said I was like my mother, Virginia.

(Headstrong. The word was like a long horse in a windy field. Her picture did not look headstrong. She was an angel now. I think she looked like Jane, only without the cracks. Jane had "EFFANBEE" in raised letters on her back. In my room, on the carved dresser, I had my mother's picture. She was quite beautiful, looking backward over one shoulder, with gay curly hair much darker than mine. I looked in the mirror and sadly saw the familiar long big face, big nose, yellow hair like a broom. I did not get any closer to the picture of my mother. I rolled up the straight hair and told people I met it was naturally curly, if there was no one around who knew to call me a liar. I told people I was adopted because it sounded better than saying I lived with my Aunt Dorothy.)

So I came down, a knowing descent to my own hell. I ate an olive sandwich in silence, not looking at anyone. They talked about Priscilla, Charlie's sister, Toby Bright's mother.

"She doesn't mind my birds' eggs and nests and rocks, but she doesn't like my snakes," said Toby Bright.

Rose swallowed her mouthful. "I don't blame her," she said. "Not one bit." Frances shuddered dramatically. I was secretly glad, since I didn't think snakes were so bad.

"I don't snake thinks . . ." I began, and they all looked at me. "I mean, snakes. . . ." But I couldn't finish, and stuffed the whole last quarter of my sandwich into my mouth with both hands. Frances laughed.

"I don't think snakes think either!" she chortled. Someday, I resolved then and there, I would become a famous snake charmer in a circus, and when Frances came to see the circus . . . but no, I could save her at the last minute and get written up in the paper even better: MISS JESSIE PRESTON, FAMOUS CHARMER OF SNAKES, SAVES COUSIN FROM GIANT COPPERHEAD.

"Snakes are very interesting," Toby Bright said seriously, looking at me. "At the Smithsonian there are thousands of them. That's in Washington." I didn't know what the Smithsonian was, but he continued, "We go there a lot. Boy, do you know they have a *whale*? A *whole whale*." He sounded very excited.

Rose nodded.

"Stuffed," he added. "As long as this house."

"Maybe sometime we'll go," Rose said absently.

Frances lifted her eyebrows. "A lot of snakes and a whale. Phew! No, *thank* you."

Toby Bright went on. "But there are millions of things to see there! There's a dinosaur skeleton. And Egyptian mummies. And thousands of things besides."

"Like a museum?" I said.

"Yes, and Jessie. . . ." But I stopped hearing what he was saying because his saying of my name echoed in my ears—

something about, I would love it. The only good things we had in our town museum were two horses' skeletons with people's initials written all over them. One was little and one was bigger. The cases indicated that they had belonged to two generals in the Civil War, but a man told me once when I was little that they were really one and the same horse: the smaller one when the horse was a pony and the bigger one when he was grown up. I fell for it, and it took me two years to get it straight.

Rose asked Toby Bright if he would like another sandwich; he told Rose about the sandwiches he had in school in Baltimore. "Peanut butter and bacon," he said. Rose and Frances laughed; I thought it sounded pretty good.

I wound my feet around the chair rung; Toby Bright told Rose and Frances about the nest we found while I stared at my empty plate so hard it made me dizzy. He said he had seen lots of other birds this morning. I was stabbed with pain that I hadn't been along, and overjoyed that Frances apparently hadn't either. If asked about the bike ride (I hoped, I feared) I tried to think of what I would say. Yes. No. I had forgotten. I would love to. Please ask me, please. No—don't think of it. I wished I could think of something to say but could not. Frances had perfume on again, a different kind today, and its horrid oily smell ruined lunch. I wished I could tell Toby Bright about my one-hundred-and-ten-day-old gum. Even with it gone, I figured it was probably the world's record. Or maybe he'd rather hear about the horse skeletons.

"Let's play something after lunch," I finally said to Frances.

"What?" She made it sound like a challenge, and I couldn't think of a single game that wasn't childish. "Never mind," she said while I was still thinking, "I don't think I want to."

I wanted to ask Toby Bright a million questions, about the

birds and the snakes, and Baltimore, and I could not think of the way to say them. After lunch I hung around as long as I could, trying to look natural, my insides jumping around as if I had swallowed a basketful of live trout. Finally, I left for my hiding place again, by my own doing no longer free in my own house (no, not mine, really). The sands of time were running out since he would leave in only a few hours. My inside life was making a lie of my outside life as I strolled, loped even, toward the kitchen door. Just as I was going out the back screen door, I heard Toby Bright say my name in a half question. In a suspended instant that seemed to take hours and teeter on the very brink of the world, I stopped and decided to pretend not to hear, and went on through the door. More than anything in the world, I wanted him to follow me, to ask me again, to kiss me again.

Something was missing. It was the sound of the buzz-bang closing of the screen door, and it was because my finger was caught on the hinge side. I yanked it out and stuck it into my mouth fast, stifling a yelp, my ears still cocked for another voice. But there was no sound except the delayed buzzy *clung* of the screen door closing, and I had no choice but to walk slowly on my way, to keep going, the afternoon swimming blue-white in my springing eyes.

I climbed the slanted ladder to the loft, cool and dark and musty, the sofa smelling of mildew and dampish, the baby carriage standing over in the corner, the doll house built of orange crates four years ago, now ruined and dirty, with doll clothes stuffed in one square room and jacks and tiddlywinks spilled all over another. My one deep sniffle to recapture all the flowing water in my nose and eyes grated alarmingly loud.

I settled on the sofa to read *The Little Lame Prince*, nursing the throbbing feverish finger. But I was too easily moved to tears, I who did not cry at books or movies. So I opened my doll clothes suitcase. The tiny mirror was still there, and a broken comb. I propped the mirror on the edge of the dirty window and parted my hair way over on one side. I spit on the comb to make the hair stay in the unnatural position, and pushed it way behind my ears. No good. They were too big. Not as big as Dorothy's (she said it was a sign of aristocracy to have big ears, and once she said my father had very small ears) but still too big to show. I looked older, my hair parted like that, so I left it parted way down but pinned with many bobby pins down over my ears. I dug up a box of face powder called Love Apple that Rose had once given us, a bunch of our old dried lipsticks, and a palette of old watercolor paints. I painted black lines above my eyes, over the top of my white eyebrows, and a black spot on one side of my chin, high up, close to my mouth. I brushed a pale sunset on each cheek, then a blue sky on each eyelid. With a dark red lipstick, I drew a river of blood for a mouth, a vampire mouth, dripping red down onto my chin. Vampires were men, so with a thick brush I added an evil black moustache. I powdered over everything for a ghastly pale look. I sat back on my heels and the effect was marvelous. As the paint dried, I wiggled my face around to break the crustiness.

Pretty soon I slid down the ladder and around back of the garage to look for broken glass. I returned to the playroom and found a flower pot with only one small chip out of it. Collecting up all the glass I could find, I drew a square on the floor with a piece of coal and spread the glass out on the floor in the square and practiced walking on it. I wanted the pledge to Toby Bright to be difficult, to hurt, even, so I had to prepare myself to face it bravely.

A while later, I went back to the book, but it was so sad

it was unbearable, and I could not concentrate on it. I heard only silence from the house. I could not just go find him. I lay around trying to think of how I could bump into him accidentally. *I would be lying down taking a nap and would awake with him standing beside me and looking lovingly into my eyes. . . .* Finally I wound up the huge Victrola and put on "The Wreck of the Old '97." It worked.

In a few minutes I heard Frances say, "She's up *there!*" Then, louder, "Jes—see! Toby's leaving and you have to come with us to take him to the bus!" *We are at the bus station, Frances and Rose behind us far enough not to be able to hear; Toby Bright turns swiftly to me, saying, I'll wait forever, Jessie, sweeping me into his arms. . . .* I leaned out the window, pretending surprise.

"Oh, I do?" But it was all lost. Toby Bright was nowhere around.

"Come *on*," she said, her back already to me.

Toby Bright was putting his black suitcase in Rose's car. He smiled at me, then did a double take and put his hand up to adjust his glasses. Frances got her eyebrows close together as if she were trying to figure out an arithmetic problem.

"Have you got the measles or something?" I didn't know what she meant. "What's the matter with your *face?*" She walked closer to me, peering. I had forgotten to wash off the paint and powder!

"Oh—God—damn!" I gasped. Frances's jaw dropped.

"What did you say?" she asked. Even Toby Bright looked surprised. A slow smile began on his face, and I could not stand it anymore. Derision? Where had they been? What had they been doing? A vision of Toby Bright kissing Frances! I reached out for support to the young peach tree by the driveway that already had little hard, green peaches on it. I closed my eyes and the world swung wildly. I was dangling by a rope from a very high cliff; I could not go up; if I let go I would fall down, down, into water so deep it had no bottom.

Against Frances's perfume and poise, her shoes and sophistication, against Toby Bright's unbearable kindness, his secret smile, but most of all against my own awkwardness, clusiness, stupidity, and ugliness, I screamed, "God damn you, Frances! God damn you! God damn, God damn, God damn!" And I flung my arms around the thin tree, sobbing *God damn, God damn,* over and over, into its rough bark that was nothing, nothing like Toby Bright's mouth on mine, while Frances and Toby Bright stood side by side outside my misery and watched me go to pieces.

Speckles of light drifted in front of my closed eyes, and I began to feel a merry-go-round beneath me, moving faster and faster. I thought Toby Bright said my name, but he did not come near, did not pat me or kiss me, though that would have been the only cure in the world. My throat and forehead were throbbing.

It was Rose, after all, who led me off to the bathroom where I stood empty and allowed her to wash my face as if I were a child again. She combed all my hair down into my face, parted it in the old place, and finished combing it.

"Come on now, Jessie." I shook my head sadly, but her strong gray hands demanded assent.

"Please get hold of yourself. You're being pretty difficult these days. We'll wait for you in the car. It's time for you to grow up a bit."

I did not answer. I watched her strong broad back as she went, and when I heard the front door close, I said aloud to the empty house, "I will go barefoot all summer for you, Toby Bright." It made me feel better at once.

I rode in the back with Frances and did not talk on the way to the station. Sunday school would be the only hard thing. And if there were a birthday party. Unless it was a picnic. When summer was over I would go to Baltimore to visit Toby Bright and say what I had done. I stuck my hand out the window to feel the cool air rush by. He would be glad. And by then I would have shoes on, and maybe my bosoms would be bigger, and maybe he would kiss me again. Rose would make me a new dress if I asked her, or maybe I could make it myself. I would like to go to Baltimore to see Toby Bright and his snakes. I rubbed my hand gently across my tender hurt cheek and sniffed the air. It smelled like honeysuckle and it smelled like rain.

Toby Bright turned around and said to me, "Jessie, I left you the field sparrow's nest. It's in my room. I have one already."

I nodded. "Thanks," I said, and tried to smile. Frances was examining her fingernails very closely.

Rose said, "Well, here we are."

Maybe I could even go to live with Toby Bright in Baltimore.

The bus pulled up, clumsy as a bear, rolling slightly from side to side, and there came a strident whistle from the air brakes as the door opened.

And then, dear God, he was gone!

3

The summer turned. One night I dreamed that all my toys had been thrown, one by one, in slow motion, into a dark well, going round and round and down and down to disappear at length without a sound, broken or lost forever, while crows wheeled drunkenly in the blue crazy sky overhead or fell like arrows, gunned down by Charlie of an August morning. We didn't play anymore, and all the dolls were put away.

Slowly we counted the bounty crows Charlie shot, and they seemed to add up to the days of summer, four, eleven, eighteen, twenty-six, finally to a hundred. My feet were hoplessly huge, like dwarves' or clowns', and not a day passed without some injury to one or the other of them.

I felt prickled when Rose would not let me keep an alligator I got at a Sunday school picnic in trade for my crippled bicycle. I had fixed it by hammering out the dents and greasing it, but it wobbled always since the wreck. I had it all arranged with Bobby Lowenstein, who arrived in a car with his mother (grinning) the next morning. The alligator, almost two feet long, grinned too.

Rose couldn't believe I had made the deal and tried to frame reasons: "Where would we keep it?"

"But you live on a farm," Mrs. Lowenstein urged. "And you just throw it a pound of hamburger every few days." Rose's eyes widened at such a waste. Me the chorus: "Oh please, oh please, oh please."

Rose and Mrs. Lowenstein finally almost angry, with breakable smiles glazed upon their lips for the duration of this, Mrs. Lowenstein finally asserting: "You probably wouldn't have to feed it at *all* out here," vaguely including in her gesture field and mountain, sky and river.

Rose saying "ABSOLUTELY NOT," while I picked a mosquito bite and thought about the monster grown huge, grown to dragon size, terrorizing the countryside but tamed to my white gentle hand. Mrs. Lowenstein backed into the car again, while Bobby still sat with the big quiet box on his lap, solemn, embarrassed, running his fingers through his hair.

I gradually found I could not sleep on my stomach anymore as I had always done, for my breasts were painfully tender. So I arranged myself to sleep differently, awoke with the covers thrown off, dreamed stories of kissing Toby Bright, woke one morning with a heaviness in my thighs and stickiness I had long awaited. I felt swollen with pride, yet could not tell Frances. I walked with great dignity that day, a lumpy bandage of cotton and gauze (along with my feet) somewhat hampering my grace. I wavered between anger—the many prohibitions I knew to apply irked me, like no hair washing, no swimming, be cheerful, rest; I had read them a dozen times in The Book and they went from page 59 to 62—and exultation: I had gotten it first. At least I was pretty sure I had; I became very suspicious of Frances, however, by afternoon. How dared she keep such knowledge from me?

Finally, in the last of afternoon I got on my bicycle and rode as if hell were on fire all the way to the airport and back without stopping, with my shirt off, the Kotex pad abandoned in the wastebasket. I had decided that ignoring it was the solution: Let it come; it was not going to interfere with me. So upon returning home, I got into a very hot bath and washed my hair and me three times. I was really very angry about it. When at supper Rose commented mildly on my unusual cleanliness I rudely told her I would bathe any time I wanted. She merely picked up her pork chop bone and gnawed it. *Common*, I wanted to say. Dorothy would have said.

While we were washing dishes after supper, Rose told Frances and me that from now on she wanted us to wear shirts all the time. I knew who she was talking to, so I hotly told her, "Mind your own business," and threw down the dishrag. I was horrified to have said it, knew I had gone too far, and spidery sweat crept down my back.

She looked narrowly at me, wiping stocky soapy arms on her apron.

"That's twice tonight you've been rude to me," she said.

"I'm sorry," I mumbled. "Can I go out now?"

"Not until you finish drying those dishes," she said. So we worked, I resentful in my silence, but eventually soothed by the familiar work.

On the night of Dorothy's death there was a new moon in the sky like a lemon peel sliver. Dr. Caldwell came and I was taken to Frances's with Rose.

About that night I remember several things especially. The

moon: wondering whether I would ever say good night to it again (I had not said good night to it for many years). My father: would Dorothy speak to him in heaven? I was sure she would be glad to see my mother. The dress: would she wear that ugly red-and-yellow print cotton one that she had on now to heaven?

Her death was so sudden I did not ever cry. I was not, to tell the truth, even sorry. I really had never loved Dorothy at all. Perhaps that is why her death came as a surprise, but it wasn't something I minded. I would miss the house, but not her.

When I thought about it afterward, I thought that the death itself should have been a thing with angels and music and light, or at least a thing with darkness, but surely not a thing so simple, in the kitchen where we were washing dishes, had always washed dishes, a thing with only blue oilcloth and a bright bare hanging light bulb that lit the whole event and never even quivered or blinked, and soapy wet hands. It should have been a thing at least more than normal. For just as I was tonight with Rose and Frances, I had been washing pots while Dorothy sat at the kitchen table to rest, sipping a cup of cooling coffee. She simply gave a low grunt, said my name with a note of surprise in her voice, and fell over to the right, knocking over the cup of coffee and spilling it on the pine table. There was no blood, no yelling, just a thin trickle of spit from her tight cracked mouth.

I did not know she was dead, and tried to pick her up, prop her back in the chair, in which she would not stay propped. She had looked so terribly undignified slunched over like that.

Suddenly, I saw Rose looking at me, and I wondered if she knew what I was thinking about. But all she said was, "Jessie, you need a dry dish towel."

Dorothy was never loose, except that once. I felt only the slack weight slumping downward, crumpling, as lifeless as a sack of vegetables, not a bit like Dorothy, usually so stiff.

And later, I felt as if I had watched the death on a moving picture screen, but had at the same time touched the dead and known it was real death, not just movie death. Even at the time, when I did not know she was dead, as I looked at her she seemed just some *thing* sitting in the chair, not Dorothy, not anyone I knew.

Most people I knew had some faint glow around their heads and shoulders, but Dorothy never had. I felt certain I could never wash off death, having once touched it, and my skin crawled to remember. I said all the spells I knew, and carefully kept a four-leaf clover under my pillow for many nights. I prayed hard for deliverance from ghoulies and ghosties and four-legged things that went bump in the night. But that was later on.

Before I knew she was dead, I looked out the window and noticed the bright slivery crescent moon. I called Rose on the telephone, told her something was wrong with Dorothy and to come quickly. I stayed in the hall. Rose came, it seemed, in seconds. As soon as she came she called Dr. Caldwell, and her hushed voice told me Dorothy was dead. I did not go back to the kitchen, but sat in the living room with Rose until Dr. Caldwell came, my hands drying sticky-soapy, finally stiff.

Frances was waiting for us, asking questions about what was wrong with Dorothy. Rose simply told her to hush and that she would explain later. I told Frances that Dorothy was dead. Frances widened her eyes but hushed. She didn't mention Dorothy to me again until much later, when she asked if I saw it and wanted to know the details. For the time being she was very gentle and kind and played all the games I wanted to play, and we fixed the kinds of sandwiches I liked best in the two days that followed before the funeral: raisins and mayonnaise, brown sugar and butter, and fried egg.

I loved spending the night. We made fondant with Rose, and separated it into different pans that we tinted different colors. The vanilla was white, the peppermint turquoise blue, the almond pink. The almond I did not like because it reminded me of Jergens' lotion.

I mentioned pomegranates one morning. There they were for supper, exotic and new. I didn't admit to anyone that I thought they tasted kind of boring. I had read about them in a story, a book of German fairy tales. It was the same book that had that strange word in it: "Frances, what does 'misled' mean?" I had asked, after trying to figure it out. I hated to admit that, at age eleven, there was still a word I didn't know.

"My-zld?" she repeated. I read her the sentence: "But then Hors-Dieter misled the princess. . . ." We decided it had something to do with love because that was where it mainly occurred. We couldn't find it anywhere in any dictionary. At the marriage ceremony at the end—everything turned out all right after all—they all ate pomegranates.

Two afternoons later I went with Rose and Charlie to the cemetery. Frances wasn't along, but had instead gone to school that day. Rose, as a treat, took me to a restaurant for lunch where, scot-free, I ordered applesauce, a chocolate milk shake, and chocolate cream pie. The applesauce was for appeasement, since I was worried that Rose would not really keep her word to let me have whatever I wanted.

After lunch we went to the funeral, I in a new coat Rose and I had picked out before lunch. It was blue and had silver buttons and a hood, and I felt very grown-up in it. I had outgrown last winter's gray; the sleeves came all the way up to my elbows and my shoulders felt squeezed. Rose held my hand while Dr. Caldwell talked.

Of all the people I met there, only one was memorable because of what she said, and I could not keep my eyes off her once I met her. Rose had been hanging onto me when she came up before things got started. She was very tiny, not as tall as me, even at the time, in a dark pink coat and a hat to match. Rose greeted her warmly and called her Willa. She called Rose Mrs. Wilson and asked if I were Jessie, and Rose smiled and nodded. She looked at me for a long moment with brown watery eyes before she took my hand in both of hers, which were white and delicate and bony.

"Jessie, I'm your grandmother," she said.

In the crowd, I could not answer, but only think, How could it be? And if it was so, why had I not known? I searched her face, delicate as an old fine teacup, for a joke, but there was only a sadness and kindness in it. I did not say anything at all and finally she let my hand go.

It did not occur to me to wonder what would happen to me now that Dorothy was gone. I was told (by Dr. Caldwell, I think or Rose, I could not remember who) that Jesus would take Dorothy to heaven, and I supposed that since she was in the gunmetal blue box, he would have to come here to get her. Although I was glad the other people were there, my curiosity was only mild. So I looked around me at the bright day, at the people who were friends and strangers, all of them grown-ups, at the trees, gray stones, and green grass, and I was pretty sure Jesus was nowhere around this peaceful place.

He did not show up, and Dorothy was finally put into the ground. In that moment a change began to take place: he was a lie, just like the rest of them, like my father, like Santa Claus. I thought, I do not need to fear Him ever again, if, in this spot, He does not come. He did not come. I even dared Him to show himself, and when He didn't, I knew that I was free.

And my grandmother, something I had never had before, became a part of the lie of it all, and so after those few moments it was as if she had never existed. When I looked again for her, at the end, I was not really surprised that she was not there.

Back at our house, the relatives had all gathered. To my surprise a good deal of the furniture was gone already. There were light places on the walls where sideboards, closets, and chests had been. The china cabinet stood open, its contents quite gone. I saw very clearly the carved wood and curved glass, and longed suddenly for all to return to normal.

Even the ruby rug in the dining room was gone. I had wanted to go away at once, to run the two miles to Frances's house, where things stayed put, and where things, things, would always be where they were then: Rose's deep blue bedspread, the green and blue and gold glass hobnail ash-trays, and the green kitchen and pantry where we made fondant at Christmas and sandwiches at lunch and tea after supper. But I did not run; I gulped and held tightly to Rose's hand.

"Bunk," Rose was saying, "this is Virginia's little girl, Jessie. This is your Uncle Bunky." The man whose look I returned was ugly and leering; the grown-ups around me talked with hard subdued voices. He held a cigar with long stained yellow fingers; his hair was long and black and curly and sprang wildly from his forehead.

"Pretty little thing," he said, his tongue going slowly round his mouth, "come here and give old Bunky a kiss." A pain, so deep and horrible I could not catch my breath, clutched at my chest. A brownish-red color glowed above his head.

"No!" I shrieked, darting away. He straightened up, laughing evilly, and I ran down the hall, up the steps, and into my room, slamming the door behind me, leaning with my back to it. At least my room was untouched, was just as it had always been, all yellow and brown and green and white. Mother's picture smiled gaily at me. I threw myself on the bed and began to cry.

My dreams came, of all the times that had been the same color and the same feel, as this day: the time years ago at Blue Hole—Dorothy, Rose, Frances.

Frances, the water is cold today. And black, I am scared. Dorothy, I want to sit here with you awhile and get warm. It's my birthday and I don't have to go in if I don't want to. Look how black the water is today. So cold. The towel feels rough and warm.

Frances and Rose are talking.

"Mother, where is the war?"

"You can't see it on this map, honey. It's lots of places."

"And where is Daddy?"

"He's not on the map either, Frances. We have a bigger one at home, and I'll show you when we get back."

"Can I see him on that one?"

"No, honey."

"Well, isn't he at the war?"

"Yes, honey, but just in one part of it. Too little to see on the map." Charlie in a uniform with a beard is what I see. He has no shirt on, and around his neck there is a necklace. Rose says it is called a dog tag.

"Now go jump into the water, honey, and don't be afraid. Dorothy will help you in. We'll have the cake in a little while. Jessie, can you blow out six candles?"

"But if Daddy's where the war is then can I see him?"

"No, Daddy's just one man fighting a little bitty piece of a

great big war. Only a little piece. Shall we have the cake now?"

It was vanilla but it tasted like chicken. Rose had used chicken fat to make it. Frances with a worried look in her eyes and a drop of water off her hair running down the side of her face. Gooseflesh on her arms, her lips violet.

"Mother, is Daddy coming home?"

"Why, of course he is, Frances. When he comes we'll all come to Blue Hole together and bring a picnic lunch. And he can meet Snowball."

"Does Daddy like cats?"

"Oh, sure. We'll all come, and maybe even bring Snowball."

"Jessie too?"

"Of course. Certainly Jessie can come too." That warms me up some.

"Mother, is Jessie's daddy coming home too?"

"Honey, Jessie's not been in the water yet. Why don't you all go in? Dorothy's there, and won't let you fall. Now go on in the water."

"Is Jessie's daddy coming home too?"

And I will not go in the water, though Dorothy and Frances do, because I'm sure there is a dead body in the water; I know it, I know who it is. It is my father, common, faceless. I do not tell them, simply say it is too cold.

Now we are in the living room of some house I do not remember.

Dorothy is talking to Dr. Caldwell, who is the new minister.

"Virginia always did such stupid things." All the cracks on Jane's doll face are close to my face.

"You know that her mother . . ." Dorothy always tells new

people about us. Dorothy is not married, does not approve of such. I continue dressing Jane, whose hair has come unglued on one side. Scalped by the Indians. My great-great-grand-mother was. But she didn't die. She married my great-great-grandfather and they built this house. All the land for as far as you could see was theirs. There was no cemetery then, only once when the cemetery was expanded they found an Indian cemetery right where they were going to make new graves. Frances and I went to see: a skeleton of a young girl, yellower than white by morning sun, the green grass around slashed down to red clay, two turquoise beads dull in the light. . . .

In a silence I look up. Dorothy and Dr. Caldwell glance at me, so I look back at Jane. I know the rules: to hear interesting things, you have to pretend not to be listening. I am good at it, have mastered the art of looking blankly at Dorothy every now and then to prove I am not hearing. Certain songs I know well enough to hum while I am listening. That fools her.

"Headstrong," she says to Dr. Caldwell, and he purses his lips on the edge of his coffee cup.

I can run like a horse, brown and glossy, slapping my legs with my hands and clattering my feet to sound like galloping.

Frances and I look for fairies and see them dressed like Robin Hood in the movies or like ballet dancers, only smaller, brown and green and thin, eating from our doll dishes, and they can give us anything we want. I want candy, any kind: a nurse's kit with candy pills; candy cigarettes to smoke; a celluloid cane filled with colored shot; bars of candy; gold tinfoil-wrapped coins of chocolate.

Mrs. Tucker calls us to come in from recess; I remember we are very late and I fear we will be closed out, but there are wild strawberries at the edge of the driveway and I must pick

them before I go in. Frances leaves me to go inside; I go to-
ward the strawberries, but arrive to find something else red
in the drive. I step toward it, but stop in horror. It is a rat that
someone has run over and its colors are exactly the same as
those of the wild strawberries. I cannot cross to the wild
strawberries on the other side of it because of the body.

I hang by a rope over a deep swelling body of pale tur-
quoise water; no land is in sight; I cling dizzily to the rope
because beneath me in the water is the body, dead, that I
may touch. My father. The water is warm and inviting, but
I cannot go in it, am deeply afraid of the even water that
swells up nearly to my dangling feet.

I awoke after that dream, two years ago now, to find it was late afternoon and Rose was sitting in the rocking chair in my room reading a magazine. The house was quiet now. Seeing me awake, she smiled and put down the reading.

"Let's go home," she said, "it's nearly suppertime. You'll live with us for a while. Charlie will come after supper to get your clothes and things." I went with great happiness, taking only *Captain Blood* by Sabatini, to read: Frances and I had a new game, Pirates, and that weekend a movie was coming we both wanted to see, *Sinbad the Sailor* with Erroll Flynn. The only trouble was, we both wanted to be Maureen O'Hara, even though I asked first. We had seen the previews last week.

Drying the dishes now reminded me of that night more than two years ago. My mother's second cousin merely grunted her forgiveness when I said, putting the dish towel across the near chair back to dry, "Rose, I'm sorry. I really am. It's the curse, that's why."

One Saturday we all went to town, Frances and I to shop and look around, with fifty cents apiece, Rose to get a permanent. We came back to the House of Beauty at the appointed time, having spent our money. We had one lipstick apiece— one of the purple ones for Frances, an orangey one for me called "Sunburst"; a glass telephone filled with colored shot for me, licorice sticks for Frances—a pleasure of hers I could not understand and felt must be an affectation, because surely no one could *really like* licorice. She claimed she did. Money burnt our hands, so we killed our last on two Japanese spun glass cats each an inch long that we had found at the dime store for ten cents.

Rose was still not finished, and the frizzly-haired girl working on her hair said, "Bet that hair gets hot in the summer, don't it?"

"Who, me?" I said.

She nodded slowly, chewing her gum slackly.

"I guess so," I said.

"Why don't you get it cut?" she asked, twisting up one lock of Rose's wet gray hair.

"I never thought of it."

"Do you both when I'm through Mrs. Wilson." Frances and I looked at each other.

"Not me," Frances said. "I like it long so I can fix it up on top."

"You can do me," I said. So my hair was changed for the first time I could remember. Before, Dorothy or Rose had said, *Tangled, awful, needs cutting;* I had submitted to three or four *k-nacks!* that would quickly and neatly remove the bottom two or three inches. But now its lanky heaviness was sheared and shaped into a cap close to my head, was wetted and pushed upward a little, and for the first time it waved, it waved! Lilly Anne said if I pushed it when I washed it the same thing would happen. I spent many hours for the next week staring into my hand mirror, turning in front of the big mirror, in the morning sun, under the hall light at night, in the window in the afternoon, admiring the beautiful waves. I vowed to put up with the curse since I got the waves. Put up with it gracefully, that is, since I suspected I couldn't do much about it, except maybe go in swimming in the Arctic Ocean.

I thought about Toby Bright all the time and was in great pain that I could not share my thoughts with anyone. Frances was distant and hateful whenever I worked the conversation around to him. So alone I wrote Toby Bright sweet letters, in code, then put them all away in a shoe box behind the books in my bookcase. Once in July I worked three days on a real letter to him. In my efforts to refine everything, to be light and "noncommital" (Rose's word for how you acted with boys in general), I ruined everything.

I got caught at the very beginning: I couldn't say *Dear* Toby Bright. I could have written *Dear* to all the people who weren't, like Bobby Lowenstein and Phillips Hepwaite, but to Toby Bright it somehow meant too much and I could not say it. After the three days, I stood back and viewed the results. It read: "Hi there! How are you? I am fine. I found a quartz chrystal, in the red field. We made mint jelly. It is not for toast, but for lamb chops. Ha! Ha! Hope to see you again sometime. I read three more Hardy Boys' mysteries. Bye for now. Do right and do Write. Truely yours, Jessie Preston." As a last touch, I changed the "Truely yours" to "Your friend," and then back again to "Truely yours," then recopied it for the umpteenth time. I had used up an entire box of pink letter paper and experimented with six different handwritings. A day later I discovered I had spelled "crystal" wrong so I had to recopy the entire letter. The fact that it lacked class was abundantly clear (how would I ever be a great writer?), so I put it in the gray shoe box with the code letters, after inking through "Hope to see you again sometime" in case I died and someone else found it.

I dreamed he was Lancelot, and I was comforted to think that Lancelot was as ugly as Toby Bright and yet so noble. I could not decide whether to be Elaine or Guinevere; Guinevere, though she got Lancelot in the end, was very hard to approve of. In my dreams, Toby Bright came to my bedroom and I let him in through long French doors like the ones in "The Fall of the House of Usher." He took me in his arms always and kissed me, and I strained my memory to recall the smell of his skin, apples and sun. I had on negligees then like the women wore in ads, and most of all I was very calm and serene, and we talked as easily as Frances and I used to. In the daytime I drew Frances out to talk about him, but she was still very cold about that. She had visited him once when she was seven, but she wouldn't talk about that, except that together they had seen a kitten get run over.

"He's just a cousin," she would say, "and besides, he had smallpox."

"Yeah," I would say, thinking: Not mine, not my cousin, no kin to me, because you can't marry cousins. The smallpox was very romantic to me: Toby Bright, sick unto death, pale beneath pale sheets, deliriously moaning, *Jessie, Jessie.* In one five-night whoosh, I read *Gone with the Wind,* scrunched down in my closet with a dim flashlight, scratching a bad case of poison ivy. *Gone with the Wind* had been forbidden, and it was the best book I had ever read.

I carved our initials, JP and TB, on a real tree deep in the woods. People in books did that but I had never seen initials in a tree really. KA was painted on the overpass on the way into town, and I figured that someone was trying to be funny, as King Arthur lived in England, and I was quite sure that they hadn't had paint in those days. The carving of our four letters was much harder than I had expected and took a long time, nearly a whole afternoon. I was afraid for a while that Frances would find it. It looked very raw and conspicuous. I rubbed some dirt in and it looked better. Where the trunk split and the branches went upward I put a penny, for luck. And all the time I figured how I'd get to Baltimore to see Toby Bright.

I walked on broken glass every day to make my vow hurt, until it didn't hurt anymore. I was both relieved and disappointed that my vow was never known, never noticed, never challenged, and the summer moved slowly in a quarter circle of bronze.

I tried to work up confrontations that would allow me to be heroic, like asking Rose if we could go to the grocery store with her (she was supposed to say, "Go put on your shoes"), but she just said, "Sure." I wiggled my feet around a lot right under her nose, but she didn't notice. I couldn't see how she didn't, they were so big. We were not invited to a single birthday party all summer long. Sunday school was closed until September. I was a terrible coward: I planned each week to suggest church, and then couldn't bring it up since I really could not figure out how to manage that without shoes. Birthday parties or grocery shopping were easy: I could always give up either if necessary and be happy in my self-denial because it was like giving a present to my love, but if *I* brought up the notion of church and it became a family outing, how could I then refuse to go?

In August Rose said one Friday evening, "Let's go to church

Sunday." She said it to no one in particular. Charlie grunted his agreement, and I stuffed a piece of fried tomato into my mouth so fast I burnt it, roof and tongue. My heart jumped fast with zest for the adventure. Could I keep faith? For several days now I had not thought of the vow, so habitual had it become. I calculated: for seventy-one days I had gone without shoes.

"Oh, why?" whined Frances, kicking at her chair.

"Oh, let's!" I said warmly, my eyes watering from the burn, before I could think to be wary. For once, for once, Rose looked upon me with approval. Charlie grunted again, his yes-tone, his mouth full of corn, and it was decided.

"Yuck," said Frances. I was happy.

After supper that night, Charlie and I went to check on the house. In the beginning we went there a lot, but now we only went once in a while. I liked going, because it was mine since Dorothy died.

Between the house and the cemetery was a wide field. In the winter only clay-colored stubble jutted out of the ground that was usually frozen, sometimes even snow-covered. The fairies that lived there slept through the winter, and the earth always reminded me of Dorothy's cracked lips, even after she was dead. But in the spring the field always came alive with crocuses and daffodils, green moss, and irises so sweet I had tried to eat them one year, and was very sad that they were not very tasty.

Every year I had waited impatiently for the summer things —honeysuckle, the Queen Anne's lace with jewels at the center and the promise that one day I would find the real jewel; the fairy wings that read W for war or P for peace; the sweet wine-berries with sun shining through. In the years that the wings had W's on them Frances and I talked about what we would do if there were war. We decided that we liked the W years better than the P years, and thought that war would be more interesting, though on Sunday in church (when we went) we prayed for peace.

One summer the willow tree by the tiny creek had been struck by lightning in August, and for the month that had remained of summer we had a house in it where it had fallen. In September when the workmen had come and chopped it to pieces and carried it away I had felt miserable, for it had been a house with a father, Frances and I the daughters. His name was William Devine. The field had looked so empty without the tree, nothing but high stiff grass and a few brittle strawflowers the red-brown of dried blood. I could not bear to stay there then, as each fall progressed, and would finally go around to the front of the house where the real world was and people walked by, and pop maple tags. Every year had gone something like that; eventually the maple tags had got all used up and I had moved inside for the winter.

The house Dorothy and I had lived in had truly been the best house in the world. Nothing had ever been thrown away in it, and there were new drawers to search all the time. Frances and I would have played there more but for Dorothy. She was nice to Frances and me only when Rose was there too; of course, when Rose had visited at the same time as Frances, that meant Dorothy had company and we had to play very quietly.

So I had mostly played alone in the marvelous dark and red and brown house with the wonderful mingled smells of more than a hundred years, with the beautiful glasses and cups (my mother drank out of them!) and pictures of people we were kin to—but not my father—and one picture of my mother when she was a little girl, holding a comb, looking off to the side, her hair very dark and curly and pulled back with a ribbon.

We mostly played at Frances's. Rose had a car and drove us back and forth. Rose made us doll clothes, fudge, fondant, even real clothes. The only trouble was, she had never liked me very much. I could tell. She liked everything Frances did.

Dorothy. She didn't like me either, and always beneath the even, tight face was something scary, something that made me anxious to be somewhere else. Her breath and footsteps and words all seemed too measured, and I feared always that without meaning to I was pushing her nearer, nearer the edge of something.

Fearful as I was, I could not seem to avoid upsetting her all the time. I tried to please her and brought her candy; but she would say I should save my allowance and then I would remember just yesterday a lecture on that subject. I would hand her a glass of milk, trying to help; but when it spilt she would remind me that only the day before she had told me about reaching.

I thought it would be nice for us to have a cat and found one, a dirty starved runny-eyed white one, just past being a kitten. In great joy I took it home and Dorothy found us in the bathtub, I still in my school clothes and coat trying to wash the cat to whiteness. The cat had to be held, I explained, because it didn't know us yet. Dorothy was mad about everything: clothes, cat, water, always doing stupid things. The kitten was put out the back door into the cold afternoon, wet and skinny, and I dared not suggest we wait until it was at least dry and give it a little milk. I never saw it again, and went to my room that day feeling very tired.

I had in the trunk in my room a tiger lap robe that a traveler had brought someone in this house once, and it was forever permeated with the smell of mothballs. That day I took it out of the trunk and, taking off my wet clothes, lay naked on it and pretended it was the cat, my cat. It was cold at first, but soon warmed up and was deliciously comfortable. I rolled up in it and when Dorothy called me to supper (cold) I awoke, wishing I could stay there forever.

It was very sad that, for all the eleven years we had lived together, the clearest single thing I could remember was this: One afternoon when I had embarrassed Dorothy while a woman was calling, I was sent to my room, and when the caller had gone and Dorothy had come looking for me, I was not there, having been drawn atticward to play in the old trunks of clothes and books and china and papers. I always thought if I looked long enough I would discover a very valuable ring or pin or treasure, so the hunt was always fun, even though I had already been through each trunk many times.

She came woodenly up the protesting stairs, her sharp face stark white with anger. Her skin, never pink, was very white and clean in the dusk, and her thin lavender lips never touched by sinful lipstick or sinful kisses, only by unsinful cold cream, were drawn together in a sharp line, with little cracks running from them like roads or rivers on a map. In the middle of the cheeks, the tiny veins ran blue. She was blue-purple and cold, just like her violet bath salts. Her black hair, which she was very proud of, was pulled back, softened only around her large ears, which, of course, she said were aristocratic. The nails square cut, her bony hands worked convulsively, like two animals apart from the rest of her, which was still. Her blue eyes stared at me through the black-rimmed glasses that sat always halfway down her perfectly straight, perfectly narrow nose.

I would have her put in the dungeon, screaming and yelling, her composure gone.

What she did was this: Standing over me there in the attic in the darkening day, she told me (after noting I was *not* where I was told to be; that, in fact, I *never* minded) that Blood-Would-Tell, that I was like my people after all, that my mother had been weak and frivolous, my father rude, antisocial, hysterical, trashy, common.

I was suddenly drenched with a burst of sweat; the word *common* was really terrible—she reserved it for the very worst people.

She said she always hoped I would be like—would not inherit—would develop some—not be like *them*—yes, *both* of them (all the time standing there before me, with fists white-colored)—that the Lord knew she had done her best, her very best, *her very best,* and she could not understand what was the matter with me.

I wanted to put my hands up to ward off the words beating against me like stones, hard and hurtful. She said—pinch-faced and looming out of the darkness behind her, night falling, the attic shapes less and less distinguishable, the window at the other end so dirty no light showed through at all, just a ghostly pale green square in the dimness, and my fear rose, rose—that she could not any longer be called to account (what did it mean?) for my temper and manners and mischief. The mild vanilla-paper smell of the attic began to make me sad.

I wished her dead, then, clearly. But she kept on talking, the words tumbling over each other: *Headstrong, irresponsible, no sense,* her voice shaking.

My body began to shake with her voice, with the slaps of her words that pricked and stung and burnt like arrows or rocks. I stood it, and in silence (that I was bad and Blood Would Tell) as long as I could; finally when I could not any longer, screamed at her that she had not ever done anything for me, and to Shut Up, pushing past her to run from the attic, her slitted eyes like claws in my back, down the screaking winding steps out onto the street, towards Frances's house, blindly, feet slapping the brick walk, by the church and Dr. Caldwell's. Dr. Caldwell! He had a light on; Dorothy would not know how to find me here. So I stopped running and walked very primly up the long brick walk, gulping down air; my heart began to beat more slowly; I wiped the perspiration from my face.

When I was quiet, I rang the doorbell, told him calmly when he opened the door that I had just dropped by for tea (it sounded like what one should say). He was having supper already, asked me if I would join in, and since it smelled good, I said yes, and together we ate beef hash and boiled cabbage.

We sat at the ends of the table, quite far apart. He drank dark red wine, and I, milk. The table was very long and brightly polished but we used paper napkins. Dorothy had often said that they were common.

Although it seemed miles to his end, we spoke of school and various matters with an ease I wondered at. Twice he asked me if I had come for any special reason; twice I said no. Twice he asked me if my aunt were not expecting me home for supper; I told him no both times. Once he excused himself from the table, and I ate two sugar lumps from a silver container on the sideboard while he was out of the room, keeping an eye on the silent swinging door, slipping back into my slick leather chair just in time. We never had candy at our house; Dorothy said it was unhealthy. Nor did we have sugar in lumps as Dorothy named that extravagant.

When Dorothy arrived to take me home, I was jolted. I had forgotten and was very calm. She looked frightened and apologized to Dr. Caldwell for my interrupting. Dr. Caldwell replied that he had been charmed by my company. He patted me kindly on the shoulder as we left.

On the way home Dorothy was agitated and said she was sorry and had not meant what she'd said; she was at times just annoyed at my rudeness, that I was not what she said, that my mother was not to be blamed. I said it was all right.

We walked on in silence until she asked, "What did you and Dr. Caldwell talk about?"

I knew she wanted to know, so I replied vaguely, "Oh, lots of things."

Finally she asked me outright whether I told him about what she said. Knowing I had, for the moment anyway, the advantage, I said clearly in the darkness, "I'd rather not discuss it." And we left it there, walking on in silence under the clear darkness. Suddenly happy, I said, "Oh, I would like to reach up and pick a bunch of stars!" *I swing from a bar in a high pink-striped circus tent and pick a star. It is like a potato chip, only sweet, vanilla-flavored. Vanilla potato chips. If I could make them . . .*

"Don't be silly," she said. "You're being silly." Angry because I wouldn't tell.

"But I *would*," I pursued. "*Really*, I would!" I loved the singing sound of my voice when I said it.

"Jessie, you cannot pick stars." Every word separate from the next.

"Yeah, I know," I told her, "but you could *try*."

"Just foolishness." I skipped ahead. Going up our walk I had to stop and spit over my shoulder when a toad hopped slanted across the path; warts were easier to avoid than to cure; curing them was a scary process that involved the full moon and the cemetery.

Bedtime; she came, sat on my bed and with great awkwardness took my hand. I left it, limp but careful, in hers, which was cold as always. Again she said she was really sorry, repeating again all the things she had already said. I watched her greasy mouth move slightly as though unsure of what it would say next. I could see the back of her head, shining and neat, in the mirror across the room. I thought she meant it but could not make myself squeeze her hand or anything like that.

Now in the dimness Charlie and I walked around the house as the rose moon rose in the dusky khaki sky, checking to be sure all the doors were locked.

"Charlie!" I said, "Look! The cemetery is closer!" He merely looked at me and nodded. "Can't you stop it?" I begged. He shook his head slightly. The awful power of the dead. Of Dorothy. Two new rows, maybe three, invaded my field like ranks of gray soldiers that would not move if you watched, but if you closed your eyes or turned your back, might leap forward in stone silence, like a spine-shivering ghostly game of "Red Light Green Light."

"It's not much closer," he said. The dew was cool and soft on my feet.

4

Sunday morning I finished combing my hair and, except for my feet, decided I looked all right.

"Jessie, where are your shoes?"

"Right here," and I patted my pocketbook. "I'm going to wait until we get there so they won't get dusty." Rose looked a bit suspicious of my beaming.

"Good idea," she said in a somewhat dubious tone. I was not generally known for my neat ways. Once there, my plan was to let Rose and Charlie go in first, then I would follow, still shoeless, with or without Frances. All my efforts now were concentrated on the quest.

But while we were still in the car, Rose said, "Put your shoes on, Jessie." I thought quickly.

"Oh. Okay." I looked at the back of Rose's neck. It relaxed. She was satisfied. Frances looked at me mildly puzzled, and her expression made a question mark. I put my finger to my lips and frowned. She decided whatever it was wasn't very interesting, and looked out the window.

"Ready?" from Charlie. I managed to leave the car last and follow them. The parking lot was sharp and hot, and I crunched down on it gladly. Just as we were entering the church Rose noticed.

"Jessie!" she whispered. I flew by her and down the aisle ahead of them. Two-thirds down, she caught up. "Here," she hissed, grabbing my arm, "you put on your shoes!" I feigned puzzlement. "SHOES!" She exaggerated the facial expression that went with it, her mouth pouching out like a pig's. I smiled helpfully, blankly, at her, shrugging. *I can't understand*, I seemed to say. Her teeth clenched, but the processional started so we all had to shuffle around and get in place, I slipping easily in first.

"Joyful, joyful, we adore thee!" I shouted. It was my favorite hymn. "Thee" was Toby Bright. I sang as loud as I could, my head back, my eyes closed. Rose had finagled past Frances, past Charlie, while we sang.

"Jessie!" It was a hissing arrow. I opened my eyes. "Where Are Your Shoes?" She glared at me. Somewhere nearby I could hear Mr. Marsh, two words behind everyone else. Rose was beaten. We sat down rustling, and I folded my hands carefully upon my lap. I perched intently, was careful not to draw or write on the program all hour long. Frances wrote one note in code: XIBU*T VQ ☾ʔ It was our oldest and simplest one and I quickly translated, "What's up?" I did not look at her, looked instead at Dr. Caldwell preaching.

Through the stained glass windows I could tell the sun was shining. Our window, the Preston window, was my favorite, with two ladies in deepest blue and red robes facing each other, and diamond shapes of gold and green around the edge. "In Loving Memory," said the top half of the lower window. On the bottom were my grandmother and grandfather's names, Andrew and Esther Scott Preston. There were two white birds carrying tiny branches in their mouths, and a tree with rosy flowers behind the two women, who were Mary and Mary Magdalene.

We sang another hymn, "By cool Siloam's shady rill, how fair the lily grows," and I thought again of Toby Bright. *At the airport. On a picnic. By the shady rill. Bringing me a lily, white and waxy and sweet-smelling. We pick watercress again, and he tells me again that he loves bare feet. I reply, I will go barefoot all summer for you.* My stomach churned with love for Toby Bright. It growled loudly, as it always did in church. I was filled with the loveliness of the day, the hymn, and my triumph. I wished I could tell Toby Bright about it. I closed my eyes and tried to keep everything just as it was, to remember for always church, its smell, this most beautiful summer, the crooning organ, the sweetness of victory. For always. Miraculously, this hymn too had words just for me; I stared in wonder at the fifth stanza, clutching the smooth rolled seat back in front of me:

> O thou whose infant feet were found
> Within thy Father's shrine,
> Whose years, with changeless virtue crowned,
> Were all alike divine . . .

And I felt crowned with virtue. I actually felt dizzy, holding tight to the warm wood pew. It was like a miracle; I pushed aside my anxiety about lunch, and beneath my feet the winey carpet squished beautifully.

The car was very hot and smelled like rubber. Rose had sent me directly to it as soon as we had finished the recessional. I tried to think. Rose stuck her head in.

"Jessie, you put your shoes on right now. We're going to lunch."

"Yes, ma'am." She watched shrewdly.

"Now." She looked at me, very mean.

"I'm going to," I said. Frances got in the back seat with me. Charlie leaned against the side of the car and squinted at the sun.

"Well?" asked Rose.

"Jesus didn't wear any shoes."

"Jesus? Well, you're not Jesus. Besides, it is my understanding He wore sandals."

"But—the hymn we sang today said . . ."

"Jessie. Your shoes, *right now*."

"I—uh—can't find them."

"Aren't they in your pocketbook?"

"Oh!—Hmmm, no, I don't think so." It was getting tense.

"Then Where Are They?" All capital letters.

"Well. I forgot them."

"Forgot them? Jessie, give me that purse." There was the slip. I cursed myself. Outside, the birds hushed. No wind blew. All nature stilled to observe my downfall. "Jessie!" she repeated. She grabbed the pocketbook, produced the black patents in triumph. "Now. Put these on." She eyed my feet. I cleared my throat.

"No," I said in a very little voice. Then I added, "ma'am."

"Why not, for heaven's sake?" she demanded, reigning in her temper.

"Well," I made an effort, clearing my throat. "They just don't fit."

"Well, just try. You're not going to spoil lunch for the rest of us and you're not going to any restaurant with no shoes." She folded her doughy arms. I could think of absolutely nothing else, so I pretended to grimace with pain as I shoved my foot into the first one.

She didn't buy it. Instead she grabbed the shoes, put them on me as if I were a baby, and said, "There's plenty of room." Satisfied, she got into the car. "And keep them on," she tossed over her left shoulder.

Poor Toby Bright! The grail was broken, the crusade was lost! Glumly I looked out the window at the dull unbeautiful summer. Only two weeks more and I would have made it. Uncomfortable, the shoes taunted me. My feet itched underneath. My arms felt particularly empty and heavy, and dangled uselessly somewhere on my skirt. *Nothing I do is right.* I ruined everything.

But at lunch I ate four pieces of fried chicken and then spotted the fortune-telling scales. In my pocketbook were two pennies and some dirty Kleenex and a dirt clod from one of the shoes. I offered one of the pennies to Frances, so that Rose to reward my generosity would let us work the machine.

"What does yours say?" I asked, savoring until the last minute the delights of learning my own.

"One hundred and fourteen pounds. Beware of people pretending to be your friends." She looked at me significantly, so I made a secret spy face at her. Then I got on the scales and put in my penny. *Bink,* went the bell of the machine, and out came the stiff little white slip of card. Quickly I grabbed it lest the spell be broken. "122 pounds," it said, "You will take a long trip soon." I was stunned; I was overjoyed; the weight was suddenly lifted.

Frances wanted to know what it said. I told her, reading the miraculous words carelessly, and added, "I wonder where!"

"Ha," she said, "probably Richmond to buy our new winter coats."

"Probably," I agreed. I called her attention to a joke of long standing with us, a sign that had been pasted on the mirror behind the cash register for as many years as we had come here. It said, "Congeal salad 15¢." We used to think congeals were some kind of fish. Now I nudged her and pointed to the sign.

"I'd like a dish of congeals—fried." Frances opened her eyes wide with shock.

"How can you *bear* to eat the poor little things? The SPCA ought to know about you!" My heart, in that moment, seemed to soar heavenward once again. That was the first moment we had shared like that in nearly three months. I wanted desperately to preserve it.

"Congealed congeals," I said. "It's the newest thing. Oh, Frances, let's play something this afternoon." But I had gone too far. Her eyes regarded me coldly.

"Mother is going to fit my new dress this afternoon," she said, "and besides, it's too hot to play." There was no mistaking the disdain she poured upon the word "play."

So that afternoon, rain threatening, I counted my money. All of it. Even the dollar in my winter hatband; even the dull blood-smelling pennies in my old Orange-Glo bank I got for nothing at the grocery store once with Dorothy many years ago. I even considered getting the penny I had hidden in the tree, but did not. It might have been bad luck.

All together, with the five dollars I had made painting the living room sky blue, I had $8.88. It was the third miracle today, after the hymns and the mysteriously right message from the machine; I knew that it was a sign that I must follow.

In the afternoon, Frances was reading and didn't want to do anything, so I played solitaire and made plans.

Around four the sky was bruised-looking and the sheet lightning began, silent and eerie. I went to the back porch and watched it, wondering if I would ever see this again, the mountains grape purple and fields glowing dull yellow until the second of the white, white lightning that came from nowhere and had no shape; even as you tensed for the thunder you knew that none was coming, and still a slight tightening happened inside your ear, and your back automatically got stiff, shoulders hunched against the imagined blow. The metallic smell of ozone was sweet and heavy on the air.

Around five, when the wind began and the leaves swirled around in square-dance fashion, and the sky fell so low the birds wouldn't fly, I went inside and tried to breathe. The house was eerie, lit by a yellow-purplish cast. It was a great relief when the rain started and the real lightning and thunder. A tree crashed down somewhere in our woods just at the storm's height; we could hear it maybe a half mile away. It was too big, from the sound, to be my tree, the initialed one with the penny.

We ate supper just after the storm, and by seven the air was cooled and stone-scented and Frances wanted to take a bike ride. So, talking hardly at all, we pedaled in the wet evening out along the road to the airport, for the last time though she didn't know it; and I tried to suck in as many of the good smells as I could. The summer had all been like that; mostly silence from Frances, all my comforts from the growing things, roses so lovely my throat ached knowing they had already begun to die at the moment they were most beautiful, honeysuckle so sweet-smelling it made my stomach churn, grass green enough to hurt my eyes, and leaves so tenderly delicate they could not possibly last.

"I wish it could be summer all the time, don't you?" from Frances. I began to agree, found that I didn't. There was snow, Toby Bright, cocoa, fire, cold places with him in my arms. I only wished it would *smell* like summer all the time. But that would probably be boring. What made lilacs so marvelous was that they were only here for about a week, and you waited for them and got ready for them, and maybe even the getting ready was better than the lilacs themselves. Lilacs were even better than the honeysuckle, which lasted nearly all summer. Maybe that was why. Maybe even friends were like that. Frances. Maybe she was always there, and Toby Bright was better because he wasn't.

Once when I was in the third grade a girl named Teresita moved to Borden and went to our school. She had black curls that were natural. Every day then Rose would come after school to pick up Frances; she usually would invite me to come play with Frances. But Teresita and I had become friends. I loved her stories about gypsies and we played gypsies. I taught her a secret code which Frances did not know, so we could write notes. Frances did not like her, but I didn't care since I did. Her house was wonderful, very warm, with the radio turned way up; they lived in the old army barracks that had been used during the war and were very decrepit now; I had never known anyone who lived there before. I was for some reason very cautious about never mentioning Teresita to Dorothy, and I never invited her to play at our house.

Teresita's mother had five other children, two very little, and the house was always lively, with all kinds of heavy comfortable furniture and the constant smell of woodsmoke and candy and cookies and Teaberry gum all over the place. The children laughed and hugged me a lot. Teresita's mother always hugged me along with Teresita when we came in, and

Teresita's father sang hillbilly songs with me when we came home. He was always there, sleeping in the big bed or on the red couch. He worked at night but never seemed to mind that we woke him up. They had about twenty cats, mostly kittens, and we could do anything we wanted. No one at Teresita's ever criticized; they just laughed a lot. Even the babies hardly ever cried, and if one did, everyone rushed to love it. They even loved me, an amazing fact I had known then, knew now, though could no longer quite believe, nor remember how it was that I had known. I remembered most of all how warm it was there; the ceilings were very low and on the bleak November afternoons their house, a section of the long barracks, was hot and friendly and full of sweet things. I loved best chewing a full pack of the Teaberry gum.

Sadly, it was to last so short a time. About two weeks after I had started going there, Dorothy got wind of it, and Teresita's house was forbidden. I suspect Rose told her on me. I was told they weren't the right sort of people, that *he* was only a night watchman, and I was not to go there anymore, as they were common. The very next day I had noticed the tawdriness of Teresita's clothes, the ill fit of them, the smoky smell that always hovered around her.

On that last day she gave me a ring I had always coveted; it was gold with a little oval purple jewel. At the time we were standing in line to use the pencil sharpener.

"I can't take it," I whispered.

"Yes, you *can*. I want you to have it. You've always loved it." It was true. Twice she had let me keep it overnight. I would wear it home, then hide it, as Dorothy did not allow me to wear rings, and admire it on my hand only in private. It was beautiful and made me feel very good. Teresita grinned encouragingly and hugged me at the waist with one arm. At any rate, I took it. And I never went to her house again, though she invited me every day for three weeks, more and more puzzled, and finally hurt. I avoided her face at school, played with Frances at recess, and went home with Rose after school. One day she did not invite me anymore, and that was that.

For some reason, I remembered Teresita for the first time in years, the best friend I had ever had. Except that it all went against the grain of lesson: that best things are things that last the longest. I wondered what had happened to the ring; I hadn't seen it for years. Teresita's family had moved away after only a short time; now I wondered where. Summer hurt too much, starting with its lilacs that were dead so soon, its roses that were gone in one day, its moment of Toby Bright. It occurred to me at that instant that I was very tired of it, tired even of the honeysuckle and the roses. It was time for a change. I did *not* wish it could be summer all the time at all, was anxious for burning leaves and red-gold color to replace the endless greens; longed for even the dull blue-whiteness of November.

We didn't stop at the airport, but turned around as soon as we got there, since we were not allowed to ride after dark.

5

I got ready: shoes, old; my first stockings, new; a garter belt that sagged and had belonged to Rose; my favorite dress, not my best; my white nylon gloves; the two bracelets that were my mother's; my Easter topcoat, red with gold buttons. In Rose's long hall mirror I surveyed myself critically (everyone had gone to bed so I was very quiet) and added a slip in case I was in a wreck and anyone picked me up. My largest pocketbook would go: it was navy blue leather, the same color as my dress by good chance, and contained the money, a bunch of Kleenex, my sunglasses, the ticket from the scales which I read again, slowly, memorizing it word by word; on the back was a smiling picture of Dinah Shore, and I planned to try my hair like hers. To all these things I added Toby Bright's bird's nest in case I never came back, and a Kotex and the elastic belt, just in case.

I had some things for Toby Bright that I had saved from the summer; the quartz crystal I had found in the clay field after a rain in July—clear, perfect, tiny; a brown speckled bird's egg, whole, that I had nearly stepped on one day because it was just sitting in the field behind the house; a nickel that said 1885 that I dug out of the front yard the day we planted winter crocuses for Rose, and a four-leaf clover I had found the same day.

I tried to think what else I might need. I wrestled with my conscience, ended by taking Rose's lipstick which always stayed on the tray in the bathroom. It was an expensive one, rose-tasting, in a swivel tube. I had several of my own, of course, but they were in the playroom, and old besides, and I didn't dare risk getting any of them. I would write Rose and tell her she could have all mine. Besides, hers was nearly half used up so it wasn't as bad as taking one nearer to new. Rose had brought a book for us from the library, *The Myths of Greece and Rome,* and I stuffed that in as an afterthought. At the last minute I was tempted to awaken Frances to say good-bye, then changed my mind, realizing in an instant of clarity that she wasn't, hadn't been, my friend for some time now. I saw that Toby Bright's visit really marked it exactly, when I thought of it, and it occurred to me that there might be some connection between her distance and all those hours, those days and nights of my loving. What was it? Could Frances love him too? At any rate, I didn't awaken her, but slipped out of the house without a sound or a sign.

The night was warm and wet; dense fog hovered in the dip where the driveway went down to the road. I forced from my mind the fear of monsters by singing to myself; nonetheless I jerked, unable to control myself, when the old oak branch, the one we scraped each time we went by in the car, loomed like a gnarled dead hand to hold me back, from the pale blue of the fog. I bitterly regretted the horror comics I had read by day and promised myself if I were spared to never read any again.

For a few moments after, I was totally alone in the silent fog that smelled like stone after rain, feeling my way as though in a dream, and I greeted the mailbox as though it were a long-lost friend. C. H. Wilson, it said. It was empty, so I turned left and began the two-mile walk to town. I looked back, but could not see the house in the fog.

My feet carried me, picking their way through the damp warmth. Once I stepped on something hard; it was an apple and I picked it up, tasted it. Exceedingly sour it was, and I tossed it down into the blackness at my feet. It bounced once and then landed softly in the weeds by the road. Once the sound of a car motor warned me to step off the road, over the ditch, all the way to the fence, and I watched as the two pale lemon-beams flared out like long cones into the damp darkness. My walking was automatic; I stumbled ahead, and the fog swirled densely inside and outside my head.

I was going to Baltimore to see Toby Bright; that was the only thing clear to me. At the same time I could not believe it was I doing this thing. My life seemed to be reopening; I would be good and pretty and pleasant and I would live in the city, someday returning to visit here.

I thought of Dorothy's funeral, of the fondant, of my father, of my grandmother, of Jesus, of a certain night long ago when I was very small.

Dorothy had carried me out to the back porch to say good night to the moon, as she often did then. It was spring and the air was clean and soft because it had rained that day. Across the air we could see the cemetery, dark and full of puffy trees, surrounded by a low black iron fence. We said good night to the moon, and a smell like new grass wafted upward on blue cellophane air. We were higher there than the tops of the other houses far off.

The cemetery was farther away than it was now, even though they moved the iron fence out nearly every year in the early spring. The stones that marked the dead people were clear here and there in the moonlight. My mother was there with our name: Preston. And doves and a cross. I said good night to Mother, who had been in heaven since I was born. Heaven: blue of our Sunday water goblets. I was the last Preston.

"Do common people go to heaven?" I had asked Dorothy.

"Of course," she said.

"Is my father in heaven too? Frances said he was dead. Is he in heaven?"

Dorothy waited a long time, made a noise in her throat, and answered, "You have a heavenly father. God is your father."

"Is he in the cemetery?"

"No, he is in heaven."

"How can God be my father?" Charlie was Frances's father. "Is God dead?"

"Of course he's not. He watches you and he knows when you are good and when you are bad." A peppermint Christmas song skimmed the back of my thoughts: "He knows when you've been good or bad, so be good for goodness' sake. . . ."

I know a secret: There is no Santa Claus. Rose told Frances. I wished fiercely for it to be unso; my scalloped tooth came out when I bit her bottom; I didn't mean it to be her bottom; my teeth just landed there by accident.

Is there no Jesus either then? "How old was Santa Claus when he died?"

Frances doesn't understand; "He didn't die," she says, "everyone knows that." Everyone but me.

"Well, then, how old was he?"

"About a hundred, I guess," she says, with a shrug, as thought it weren't important.

I swung my feet. Some of the rain from the afternoon had made a puddle just in front of where Dorothy was standing with me. It was still as glass and clear as a mirror. The reflection of my feet was large and grotesque, practically blotting out the rest of my body. I kicked slowly at the reflection, watching the mimicking shape in the water jerk an uneven arc inside the frame of dry enclosing the puddle.

"What does God look like?" thinking red suit, white beard, presents.

"You can't see Him but He is good." That was okay. You couldn't see Santa Claus either.

"Can I say good night to God?"

"May," Dorothy said.

"May." To play the game. *"May I say good night to God?"*

"Yes." Maybe God is Santa Claus. I think Jesus was my father. They were thirty-three. My mother was twenty-three.

"Can He see me all the time?" Dorothy shifted me to the other arm. I could only see the fairies sometimes, just as they moved behind things. Little, thin, with ballerina skirts and wings. I found the wings later with Frances, though Dorothy said they were locust wings. Looking down, I could not see my feet anymore in the water, only the moon.

"Of course," she said.

He was the size I was to the fairies.

Poague's mailbox appeared in the dark. It was the halfway point to town. A soft whinnying nearby made me remember a horse in a windblown meadow and the word *headstrong*. The air was silver, and in the windless fog I caught the mingled ammonia scent of cows and field mint, harsh and blue. I peered at myself in a watering trough by the side of the road, and my face was ghostly gray and frightened. Fear stirred in my head, a sense of awe that I was doing this, and a momentary desire to run, run, back to my bed, my things; I even stopped for a moment. But I needed to go to the ocean, to the city, I needed to hold somebody, and I needed to tell somebody I loved Toby Bright. Just like that. I said it aloud in the haunted air: "I love Toby Bright." Nothing happened, and there was only the fog to hear.

I reflected that in leaving so, I was changing my whole life, an awesome thing I had not fully considered. Whether I came back or not, everything changed at this point. I knew it was all still reversible, and I hesitated, considering a quiet return to my place in the Wilsons' house, though it had never been my house. I had just a vague hope that somehow Toby Bright and I would live happily ever after. I would have to learn to cook a lot of things. I would probably have to come back eventually, for a while anyhow, to get my things. I did not know if things really could turn out like they did in the movies, but there was something inside that nagged at me that it could not be.

Only last week, in the newspaper there had been the long story of a man I would have liked to know. I had wanted ever since to go to the jail to see him, though of course I had not, knowing Rose would not understand. I didn't know how to visit people in jail, anyway, never having done so.

The man must have thought for a long time about his plan, more than I did by a long shot, and on a Tuesday morning a couple of weeks ago, he'd gone to Dunlop's Hardware (spelled *Hdwre* on the sign out front) and bought a small pistol and a box of ammunition. On Tuesday afternoon at about two o'clock, closing time, he had held up a branch bank in Courtland, forty-five miles away, and gotten five thousand dollars in cash. He had, as a matter of fact, asked for five thousand dollars exactly. He had then driven to the next county, to a town thirty-six miles farther away, and purchased for cash a light purple (lavender, it said in the paper) Cadillac convertible, and, at a store only a block away, an expensive electric guitar and amplifier. He stopped at the A&P for a six-pack of Dr. Pepper. Courtland did not have the last thing he needed so he drove his new car to Washington, D.C., and bought that—a light green sequined suit with an embroidered guitar on the front. He spent the night in Washington, D.C.

After driving around in the lilac-colored Cadillac for most of a day, he returned to the town where he'd bought the guitar and the automobile and the Dr. Peppers, and checked in at a Quality Courts Motel under the name Ever Summer. (His real name was Dooly Hickman.) He called for ice to be brought to his room, and then he locked the door. Because he did not think he should throw away the twenty-seven envelopes that had on them the name of the bank he had held up, he tore them up in little pieces and flushed them down the toilet. The toilet became stopped up. He asked the desk to call a plumber. When the plumber came, he unlocked the door in his green sequined suit and let him in. When the plumber was through, Mr. Ever Summer thanked him and showed him out and locked the door again. And when the police arrived, not quite thirty minutes later, they could hear the sounds of someone trying to learn to play a very loud instrument. They surrounded the motel and then two men crashed in through the door. Mr. Ever Summer was sitting on the blue chenille bedspread drinking his third Dr. Pepper with ice, still dressed in the sparkling suit, playing two chords over and over on the electric guitar, with the amplifier turned way up. He offered no resistance to the police, did not even seem surprised to see them.

That was something like I wanted to be. I almost thought that jail wouldn't matter as long as you got exactly what you wanted first. And so I kept going, on into the milky blue darkness. When a cat darted out of the night across the road in front of me, I jumped back, startled. But I would go on, though already I felt horribly unprotected: there was no one to look after me, and I ached deeply with a loneliness that had no object, only maybe Toby Bright. I was momentarily shocked at the deception of love; I ought to be able to say, Frances, I love Toby Bright. Toby Bright, I love you. I would say it when I saw him. It was not fair, not true, not to say it.

The bus station lighted up like a castle became apparent through the diminishing layers of fog, and I was surprised to have got here so fast; it was as if I had just closed the front door and been magically brought here in a split second through some night-blue tube, like what happens in dreams; and only in the uneven pressures still echoed on the bottoms of my feet did I know I had walked the two and one-half miles.

I cleared my throat in a very businesslike manner until the man behind the counter, a newspaper over his head, woke up. I did not think he was very businesslike. On the long bench by the door, a man slept in blue jeans and an undershirt, and at the far end of the bench another man lay, his head back on a duffel bag, his mouth opening and closing slowly in tremendous snores.

"What time is the next bus to Baltimore?" I asked.

"Two ten," he glanced at the clock on the wall behind him.

100

It was twenty minutes until two. "Washington. Change there. Seven twenty bus into Baltimore, unh . . ." he looked over his glasses to consult a list scotch-taped to the counter, "eight twenty."

"Okay. I'd like a ticket, please."

"Round trip?" He eyed me suspiciously.

"Yes. I mean, no. Just one way. I'm going to visit my grandmother." His eyebrows relaxed. He opened a drawer, pulled out a narrow purple paper slip, punched it twice, and handed it to me. He had punched B-don and B-mre. In between were the abbreviated names of many places.

As I studied it he said, "Two fifteen." I paid him and asked for two Mars Bars. One was never enough, was really worse than none at all as it left me with such longing for more. I ate the first one fast in the happy knowledge that the second was still to come, savoring every mouthful of pebbly sweet melty chocolate, hard nut that cracked satisfyingly, rich malty flavor, and my jaws ached in response to the consistencies and tastes. I put the second deep into the pocketbook, and felt very proud that I could keep it there. One thing I had always admired about Rose was that she could keep the same package of Life Savers in her purse for months sometimes, eating one only occasionally. I always ate the whole package right away, and thought it a mark of great maturity to be able to *keep* candy. I stood it as long as I could, dying to show or tell someone the Mars Bar was still in my pocketbook. At two exactly I ate it.

The bus smelled of cigarette smoke and businessmen, and along the aisles people sagged into the gray plush seats. I picked an old lady reading a book in the pearly beam of the overhead light and asked her if I could sit beside her. She nodded, patting the seat. Just behind were two more women;

all three looked vaguely like schoolteachers. The men on the bus all looked sinister or shabby; I felt safe surrounded by the comfy women with their plain smells. Old ladies are the only people in the world who don't have smells. They just don't smell like anything at all. Or maybe, sometimes, faintly like lard. I sneaked a look at the book the old lady was reading; it was called *Your Key to a Richer Life*. I settled myself with my feet under me on the seat and got out *Myths of Greece and Rome*, but it was not as interesting as hers, which I kept snitching looks at. She finished a chapter; I saw that the next one was called "Christ's Horn of Plenty." I asked her what the key to a richer life was.

"Jesus, honey." I was disappointed that it wasn't more exciting. She looked me over closely. "Are you saved, honey?"

"I don't think so."

"That's terrible! Do you say your prayers and go to church school and worship the Lord?" She seemed anxious to know.

"Oh, sure," I said. The praying part wasn't true, but I had tried telling people the truth—that praying wasn't any good and that Jesus and Santa Claus were both as dead as run-over cats—and I knew that wasn't the thing to say. Sunday school and church were okay, especially the singing.

"But you're not saved?" Without waiting for my answer she continued, "Let me tell you something. My husband wasn't saved, either. He died without repenting. Not saved." Her chin trembled. "And *you* know what *that* means." I assumed I was supposed to, so I nodded. "Honey, you pray to Jesus and get down on your knees and beg forgiveness. It don't come all at once; you got to have patience."

"Patience," I repeated. She nodded vigorously. Her chin was under control again.

"Patience. It says so in the Bible. You take Job now." I

thought of the man suffering: Toby Bright with smallpox sitting cross-legged outside a tent with a tornado talking to him, draped in a white sheet to cover his scars, looking solemnly at the funnel cloud through his thick glasses. The woman was saying, "Job was in the belly of that whale for nine days, honey. He had to have patience." She was deeply engrossed in the story.

"You mean Jonah?" I said in a little voice.

"I mean what?" she asked. "*Patience*, honey, prayer and patience. My poor husband wasn't never saved, never knew Jesus Christ himself." She looked out the window into blackness. I nodded.

"Yes, ma'am," trying to get comfortable. My bottom hurt whenever I sat for very long, so I moved my feet to a more comfortable position and got ready to read my book. My seatmate sighed significantly and returned to hers. I began reading about Zeus and Hera.

"You like those stories, honey?"

"I don't know yet. I just started. It's about gods and goddesses."

"They're heathen, honey," she said, darkly. "There's only One God. Does your mother know you're reading that?"

"She's dead," I said. I fiddled with my bracelets, added, "These are some of the family jewels."

"Honey, who put you on this bus?" She looked so suspicious I became alarmed.

"My grandmother."

"But you said you were going to visit her. I heard you tell the driver." She was shrewd.

"Yes. My other grandmother. I have two of them." I was as shrewd as she.

"Well." She nodded, still sad. Suddenly she turned to me

with a sharp look. "You're not Catholic, are you?" I shook my head, no. "Well, thank goodness for that!" and she settled herself to discover the Key to a Richer Life. I went back to Cronus, whose manner of getting rid of his children horrified and fascinated me. Frances would love this, I knew; I would write her a letter and tell her about it.

After a while my book dropped onto my lap. Baltimore was north, and therefore cold. I wondered if I would learn to ice skate in Baltimore. Blades flashing, I skated holding hands with Toby Bright, like Sonja Henie in the newsreels. BORDEN GIRL WINS SKATING CHAMPIONSHIP. My eyes felt very heavy and for a moment I could not remember where I was. I watched the book slide in slow motion from my lap and decided not to catch it. *I walked down a narrow street with very high buildings on either side, looking for something I had lost. It was sunset and voices drifted down to me, droning voices. There were no side streets, nowhere to go but straight on. When I looked up, the houses leaned toward each other, seeming to stare from their windows like vacant skulls. No one lived in any of them. I was looking for something I had lost, not on the ground, but somewhere in the darkness ahead, maybe something I never had. (I wanted someone to come, but when I tried to call my throat ached and no voice came out.)* Once or twice I woke up as the bus halted, screeching and braking, jolting me like a Raggedy Ann, and then slid once again into the easy water of sleep.

"Honey!" I felt she had said it several times before. "Washington! Is this where your grandmother is picking you up?"

"No. Baltimore, I have to change to another bus."

"Do you have a suitcase?" she asked, getting across me to the aisle.

"No. Just my pocketbook."

"Well, if you're sure you'll be all right. . . . Don't forget your prayers, honey." I nodded, trying to get my eyes unclouded, and followed her off the bus into the steamy morning smelling of trucks.

My legs were jellied with sleep, and my mouth tasted sour and dirty, so I looked around for a ladies' room. It was very busy and crowded for six thirty-five, the time registered on the huge clock. I was cheered and comforted by the presence of so many people. I saw a sign that said "Restaurant" and headed for it, sat alone at the green salt-flecked counter, and drank three cups of cocoa with two doughnuts and four pieces of toast with melted butter and grape jelly from little plastic packages I had to peel. My conscience began to hurt me at this point, and I quickly ordered some apple juice for my health. A lady sitting next to me, huge and rustling, pointed a fat finger with a blue ring at the pot behind the counter.

"If that's coffee, I'll have tea. If it's tea, I want coffee." She spoke with an odd accent, like people in English movies.

"Where are you from?" I asked.

"Devon," she said angrily.

"Oh, that's near where I live!"

"Are you British?" She seemed really mad that I might be.

"No, I'm from Borden. Devon's just ten miles." She gave me a long cold look that slid down her long nose like a glacier.

"It must be a dif-rent Devon. It cahn't be very much. I'm British."

"The same as English?"

"Yes!" The word was final, accompanied by a glare.

"Oh. Are you going to Baltimore?"

"No."

"Where are you going?"

"Elsewhere," she said very firmly, and put a paper barrier between us. I felt rebuffed, but it didn't really matter.

"What language do horses speak where you come from?"

She gave me a look to wither the strongest tree, and called furiously, "Waitress, where is my *tea?*"

Suddenly, I leapt up, remembering the time. The clock said seven sixteen, and as I was running from the restaurant, something jerked me to a stop, from behind, ungently. It was the nursey-looking waitress, who said menacingly, "You didn't pay." She was too brightly lipsticked and eyebrowed. Her nose was thin with prominent tendons and veins, a little line running from the jawbone up to the ear; her mouth was set unpleasantly. I knew I would remember this face, just so, for a long time; I could remember faces and voices of people I didn't know very well; could never conjure up Dorothy's voice now, or even Frances's when I was not with her. For an instant I tried to remember Frances's face, but only brown eyes, brown hair, came to mind. Would I recognize Toby Bright when I saw him? I struggled with the deep pocketbook. Seven eighteen, the clock said.

"I didn't mean . . ." Several heads were turned in our direction. As I scrabbled around in the dark cave of the pocketbook I felt the field sparrow's nest and went more carefully. My fingers made contact with one of the dollar bills, and I pulled it out disgracefully wrinkled and gave it over into the red peeling palm. "I forgot my bus," I explained; "I have to catch a bus," avoiding her eyes with their black smeary pouches and the tiny red lines all through them. She didn't say anything, but with aggravating slowness reached into her apron pocket and came up with two dimes, which she dropped like dead things into my hand. I was angered that she wouldn't believe the truth, and I hated her painted face. So I turned my back upon her with Scarlett O'Hara dignity, and looking straight ahead, I left, walking as grown-up as I could.

The man at "Tickets," bald and fat, looked down his nose, drew his finger along the book, flipped a page.

"Ten twenty the next through."

"Ten twenty!" I fought down a rising panic. By then Rose and Charlie would probably discover where I was (my heroes could have done better at covering their tracks) and would ruin everything. Still embarrassed, I could not go back into the restaurant, so I stood outside it. More than three hours! My eyes burned, I pushed my hair back and tried to think.

I could sightsee, but I didn't know how to go about it. I remembered about the Smithsonian and thought how fine it would be to go there, then tell Toby Bright. But how could I get there? I went to the ladies' room where to my delight I discovered a vending machine that had wonderful little packets for ten cents each. I bought an eyebrow pencil, a compact, even one of the tiny lipsticks, rose. I spent two more dimes on tiny bottles of hand lotion and gardenia toilet water. I was overjoyed at the tiny things, and I even loved pulling the plungers on the machine. I washed my face with pungent green soap and set to work. I went back and spent a final dime on a comb since I had forgotten to bring mine. There were mirrors in front and behind, and I could see myself over and over and over again, finally fading into the bottle-green water of the mirrored distance. By eight o'clock I was delighted with the transformation. I was beautiful.

As I left the ladies' room I spotted the glass doors and the signs "To Street" and "To Taxis," and I suddenly knew how I could go sightseeing. Because of the movies I had seen, I knew what to do in a taxi. After purchasing a package of Life Savers, I got into the back seat of the taxi parked just outside the door and said, "Smithsonian, please." The driver, cigarette dangling, blond, curly-haired, big ring on his right hand, nodded. The radio was playing "My Lord Keeps a Record." "That's my favorite song!" I told him. He turned all the way around to look at me, and his eyes were blazing blue, his eyebrows white-blond, curly. He had on a light khaki windbreaker.

"No kidding?" He sounded impressed.

Just then a very pregnant lady walked directly in front of us, and he jammed on the brakes. I jolted forward, bumping my head on the back of the front seat. He leaned out the window. "Jesus, lady," he yelled, "you can get knocked *down* too!" He ran his big hand through the curly hair and whistled between his teeth. I rubbed my forehead hard. The lady had given him a sulky look and was harrumphing away awkwardly, heavily, down the sidewalk. I was very pleased. It was like something they said in the movies.

"That was very close," I said.

He turned and looked at me, frowning. "Sorry," he mumbled.

"It's okay," I said. Carl Storey was still singing, so I joined in, singing along with the chorus.

"That's real music," he said. "You sound good; you ought to be on the radio." Nobody had ever said anything like that to me before. I didn't know how to answer.

"I was once. I won a quiz show."

"That's great. What did you have to answer?" I told him. "Hey. I wouldn't have known that myself," he said.

I decided to return the compliment: "I bet it's fun driving a taxi and listening to the radio all day."

He turned around again, giving me a puzzled look. "Oh, it's all right," he said. "Better than being a CPA, I guess."

"What's that?" He gave me another one of those questioning looks.

"A count," is what I heard. A pigeon burst up from the slick street.

"Were you ever one?" I asked, sitting on the very edge of the back seat.

"Yeah," he said, "I used to be." I was dying to ask all about it, but sensed that it might be impolite, like asking rich people what it's like to be rich. I was thinking about it when he said, "I do some writing now and then, but I like to eat too."

Before I could stop myself I had said, "I'm going to be a writer."

He laughed. "Good for you! What are you going to write?"

"Books, if I can. I'm terrible at letters. Things like *Gone with the Wind*."

He laughed again.

"What do you write?" I asked.

"Poems," he said, "but no one buys them. They're apparently not very digestible. It's a hobby." And he made a sad clown face. Goats were the only things I knew that ate things like books.

But then I thought of a wonderful thing to say. "I guess you have to eat your words!" I told him.

He tossed his head back and laughed easily, his eyes closing up to slits. He drove through a puddle, flushing it to a gray lace fan that folded around the front of the car. The pigeons flew up from the street as we splashed them or came too close.

"When you write, do you ever write about pigeons?" I asked. He looked surprised.

"Yes," he said, "as a matter of fact, I do. At least, I did once."

"What did you say about them?"

"Hmmm. Let's see. How about:

> Now are pigeons
> Feather-giddy
> Rising in spirals
> To pigeon-gray dusk
> Descending to silence
> Of fountains."

I could see it as he said it. I closed my eyes; they burned. "Say it again." He did, and there were goosebumps on the backs of my arms. "It goes up and then down," I said. "Just like pigeons." He nodded.

"When do you write?" I asked, somehow unable to imagine him at a desk. He was easier to imagine in a field, carrying a gun. "I mean, if you have to drive people around all day . . ." I could feel my flesh unloosing its clutch upon itself.

"Not much for the last two years," he said.

"Two years!" That sounded like forever. I sank back upon slick leather. We were stopped now, part of a long line of cars, occasional drops of rain pelting the windshield with soft explosions. He leaned back, his right elbow back on the seat, and looked at me in the rear-view mirror.

Suddenly he brightened up. "Listen," he said. "It's Ray Price. You like Ray Price?"

"Sure," I said.

So he turned up the radio and punched in the cigarette lighter. It was another number I liked, "City Lights," but before I could say anything, he asked, "What building?"

"The Smithsonian."

"Yeah, but what building you want?"

"I don't know," I said. "Is there more than one?" Toby

110

Bright didn't tell me that. I decided that I'd better level. I leaned up over the front seat. "Listen, I've never been there before. I'm not from here." That made me feel better. "But I want to see the whale and the dinosaur," I finished. He jerked his head over his shoulder to look at me, and his eyes crinkled up, amazing blue, like amazing grace. They made me feel dizzy for a moment, and I had to think quickly where I was, what I was doing. Afternoon? Morning? Pigeon-gray dusk? He was saying something.

"How old are you, kid?" I pulled everything together, forced my eyes to focus on his face.

"Sixteen," I said.

At first he narrowed his eyes and pulled his white eyebrows together. Then, to my delight, he said, solemnly, slowly, nodding, "Just about what I figured." He took his cigarette out of his mouth and flicked it out the window.

"Look," he said, "I can take off awhile. Maybe I could show you the Natural Science Building." I hesitated; all the things I knew about strange men, men you didn't know, crowded my mind; I searched the faces there; there were none this nice. He was looking at me so earnestly, his white eyebrows raised slightly. I tested my memory to see if there was anything bad about taxi drivers. Nothing but a safe feeling. Poets? I had never met one until now. The only one I was very familiar with was Robert Service, and I had always thought he was like Robert Mitchum—hard on the outside, soft on the inside. I had to decide.

"Okay," I said. "That would be very nice, if you don't mind." He stuck his big hand with gold hairs springing out of the back of it over the seat.

"Bob Brunelli," he said, and smiled. "You can call me Bill Wordsworth if you want to."

I gathered that it was a joke, but I didn't get it, so I just said, "I'll call you Bob, if that's okay." The hand was still there, and I suddenly saw that I was supposed to shake it. I did, and it was firm-dry-warm. I wished I could keep holding it, and was stabbed by a sudden fear. Home seemed very far away. I pulled my hand back.

"Well?" he asked.

"Well what?"

"I have to know your name or I won't be able to call you anything but Sylvia."

"Oh." I thought a moment. "Frances Wilson." It just came out, sounding very strange; the instant it was out I knew I could not change it.

"Well, Frances," he said, "if we can find a parking place on the mall, we'll go in." He reached over and turned the handle back on the meter, and we swung onto a double street divided by a grassy green strip. "Keep your eye out for an empty place," he told me. I was delighted to play the game, seeing there were no other cars along either side except for two. Pretty soon we were parked, practically the only car in sight. It had stopped raining. "It's getting so you never can find a place to park," he said, clucking his tongue. "We'll just stop by the White House on the way back and ask to speak to the president about it."

"Yes, he asked me to stop by while I was in town anyway." I said. "He's an old friend of the family's." Bob laughed and looked at his watch.

"Just opening," he said.

Getting out of the car I caught a glimpse of myself in the rear-view mirror and was wondrously surprised at the new me. I dabbed at my short yellow hair and whispered to myself, Toby Bright, I am coming to see you; Toby Bright, I love you, my confidence soaring like a white bird in the morning air. The day was warming up so I left my coat in the taxi. Sunlight as thin and yellow-gray as lemonade tried to penetrate the wet city. Brakes screamed periodically, and airplanes flew very low over our heads. Bob looked at me smiling.

"You've made the sun come out," he said. "We are all very grateful." I felt myself grinning, and I stood as straight as I could.

"That's beautiful," I said, and I felt better than ever in my life before. The ground of the street shimmered and shone, and I might have been walking on water.

"I can pay."

He laughed at that. "No," he said mocking-serious, "let me." I figured this must be a date; no one had ever paid my way before. "This is my mother," he solemnly told the yawning man standing uniformed inside the door. "Don't mothers get in for half price?" The man didn't answer, only pressed something in his hand that clicked. I knew you weren't supposed to watch; at least in movies girls didn't.

"How much was it?" I asked inside. He laughed at me and showed me his big palms.

"I'll have to come clean. They don't charge you here." So it wasn't a date after all. I grinned anyway. He looked amused.

"How old are you really?"

"Oh, sixteen," I said, very firmly. But I couldn't stand his eyes that looked as though they knew everything. "Or at least I will be *very* soon." He shook his head.

"You belong in a nursery rhyme." He swept his arm around, indicating the whole building. "Welcome, child of light, to the realm of shadows. To quote a great but unknown poet. Come, let us shed light down the valleys of the past."

"I just love the way you talk," I told him.

It was like dreaming. My head throbbed and my eyes still burned. The walk to the bus station seemed ages ago. My vision was filled with the dinosaur bones at last, huge, awesome, cracked, and I tried to clothe the crazed bones with living flesh, but could not see the color.

"Blue," he said, as if in answer to the question I had been thinking. "A sort of grayish, greenish blue. Don't you think so?" He seemed to seriously want to know what I thought. I nodded. It was completely satisfactory.

"I think this is what dragons looked like, don't you?"

"Undoubtedly. If you'll just stand aside, I'll slay him, fair lady." I whirled around with delight.

"I'm Maid Marian, and you're Robin Hood!"

"My dear lady, this is no time for conversation. If you'll just hide behind yon greenwood tree, I'll spare you the gory sight." I hid my eyes with my hands while he said, "Take that! And that! Avaunt!" The room became deep forest; green sunlit trees bloomed instantly as the world spun back centuries to that purest of times. Suddenly there came a hiss in my ear, a hand upon my arm: "By jove, it's the sheriff of Nottingham! But I got the dragon. Fair lady, let us be off!" I took away my hands, and he glanced toward the door of the room where a fat bald man stood looking down into a low case of fossil bones, his face puckered in concentration. "He hasn't seen us yet; we may still escape unnoticed!" So we moved like sneaky spies behind a post and on into another room, where I discovered I was breathless as laughter filled my insides like water bubbles in a teakettle.

I stood very straight, and suddenly was struck by the thought: I am happy. I had never realized such a feeling of joyful, calm sureness, and here, in the midst of a strange city, with a blinding headache, on a morning like no other I had ever known, not even like any I had ever imagined, I was *happy*. The word itself had weight, mass, warmth, as we walked through this palace of objects, everything I had ever wanted to see. At this moment Bob was showing me a giant bird, a California condor, whose wings spread seven or eight feet, and without warning, I felt tears begin their ticklish course down my nose, fall *plap* on my bosom, my hand. He looked at me in astonishment. But the bird was beautiful, glistening white, like an angel, and I was *happy*.

"What's wrong?" he asked, sounding alarmed. And his face was so kind I could not bear to look. I looked instead down to where my hands were jumping all over my skirt.

"Nothing, really nothing," I tried to sound as if it were true. At least I was able to shake the tears out of my eyes and laugh. For a long instant he looked at me without saying anything. Then: "Women," he said, shaking his head, looking at me mock-disgustedly. "They always get emotional about *killing* things. It was just a dragon." And he rolled his eyes.

"It wasn't that," I sniffed. "I don't know what it was."

I imagined Toby Bright in this room, looking very closely at all the birds. I looked for a field sparrow, but couldn't find one. Then I saw an odd thing: in a case, a bird labeled "Whippoorwill." "That isn't a whippoorwill," I said.

"Sure it is," he replied. "Lots of them in Tennessee."

I stared at it a long time. I had heard whippoorwills all my life, had imagined them just out of sight, like the fairies had been, under damp ferns on pine-strewn floors, exotic green, pale, sherbety, and big: tall as cranes, silky, friendly, willing friends if I could only find them, light and clean, standing with one foot bent up beneath, nothing like this brown bird lowly and speckled, but a proper possessor of that honey-sweet, silence-stopping song. Finally I turned away. Bob was staring at me.

"Is that really a whippoorwill?" I asked. "Aren't there any other kinds?"

"No. Just this kind." I wondered if Toby Bright knew what whippoorwills looked like, and felt a little bit betrayed for a moment.

I saw myself in glass cases, and I saw Bob looking at me. We examined fish and fish skeletons, fish turned to stone or imprinted on rocks, their spines indistinguishable from ferns —and finally came to the whale! The whale Toby Bright told me about! It was inconceivable, so huge it seemed to swell wondrously until it was the biggest thing in the whole world. I told Bob the story about the woman on the bus and Job and the whale. He'd never heard a better story, he said. He might write about it, he said.

"Why did you stop writing two years ago?" I asked. He shook his head and stuck his chin out like he was not sure but trying to remember.

"Over two years. I got high blood pressure, I couldn't sleep, I was drinking too much, my wife was getting to me," (why did this seem like a blow in the stomach?) "and I was only thirty. I started going to this shrink." He glanced at me. "Psychiatrist," he added. "Wealthiest guy in Memphis, from what he charged. Very exclusive; only took six patients at a time."

I was not certain what a psychiatrist was. I thought it was a doctor of some sort. But you didn't go to a doctor about things like that. Bob looked at me, making a snooty face, rolling his eyes first to one side and then to the other, just the way his windshield wipers had moved.

"The trouble was, all he told me was things I already knew. He told me I had high blood pressure, told me I couldn't sleep from nerves, and that I drank too much. Told me I was all messed up. He never told me anything I didn't already know." He glanced at me, giving me a wry grin. I closed my eyes for a second, and the burning was worse. He was still talking, and I pulled myself back to listen.

"He used to give me the last appointment in the afternoon, five o'clock. When I got there the building was always deserted. He was on the fourteenth floor, with this sea foam green waiting room and black leather chairs and things. I was sitting there in the waiting room one night, reading a magazine, about five, trying to decide whether this was all a waste of time and money. Funny thing, I had the money then." Again he chuckled and shook his head.

"The janitor came in to clean up. 'These guys,' he said to me, jerking his head toward the doctor's office, 'what do they know? Can't cure anything by going to them. You know what's the trouble with you guys?' What do you think he said?" he asked me, tossing the question over his shoulder.

"What?" I asked.

" 'You think too much.' That's what he said. 'Lazy, just lazy. Never do anything but sit around and think. You know what you oughta do?' I said if I did I wouldn't be here now. 'This,' he told me, and he shook his broom right in my face. 'Work. People work like they used to do they'd be just fine. People think too much these days. He don't know *nothing*,' and he sort of jerked his head toward the psychiatrist's office, dumping the last ashtray into his can. After he left, clattering the broom and cans down the hall, I just sat there for a while thinking. And then I left. Next day I sent the guy a check for everything plus the session I'd missed the night before. The day after that I got a job driving a truck. I did that for a while. Spent two months in Greece. Then I came to Washington and got this cab." We were walking up some steps as he told me this. Suddenly he grabbed my arm.

"Look!" he said. "Pianos!" I saw them, a whole roomful, all in cases, wood and black and yellowed ivory, and at moments everything was sharply outlined in pale blue shining light. Bob's head was edged in silver-blue, and there was some kind of light upon his face whenever I looked. Even rapid blinking would not take it away.

He showed me a yellow cracked photograph of an awkward scrawny boy, bony as a starving dog, in shorts and a T-shirt with heavy white-blond curls, on a sidewalk, somewhere in the South, as palm trees fringed the upper corners of the snapshot; a frame house in the background was where he took piano lessons. He played the piano, had gone every Saturday to practice for seven years, free because he was poor.

"Why did you go to Greece?"

"What made you think of that?"

"The pots." I pointed.

"I don't know. It kind of seemed like the beginning of everything. I wanted to go back to the beginning. I thought it might straighten me out to go back to the beginning." I wondered if I could do that. The cemetery was the only beginning I knew. "Can you understand that?"

"I don't think so. What did you find out?"

"That it wasn't the beginning at all. That it's not out there. It's right here, where it's been all along. Inside." He tapped his chest with his finger. "I guess that's why you can't ever escape it. That's why I came back." I thought a moment.

"Do the horses in Greece neigh in Greek?" I tried to ask in a way that might have sounded as though I wasn't really asking.

"I didn't see any horses. But the donkeys do—I'm telling you the truth: I didn't understand a word they said."

We entered a small room of paintings, old, mysterious, dark paintings of ships and men and glasses of wine and naked women. I tried to store them all in my brain. All beautiful. When I looked too long at one, the blue-white light interrupted, trembling upon whatever I was trying to see, and I had to look off to the side a bit in order to see the thing, an old trick I learned about stars sometime a million years ago. I thought I could remember everything, but all eluded me almost as soon as I stopped looking.

"Look, Frances!" I reacted each time with surprise, and was reminded to stand tall, smile beautifully, be green and cool. I could still dream the green whippoorwill.

I stared fascinated at the closed clay-red face of a mummy who died three thousand years ago, but the mummy was here and now.

Bob told about how he had once worked in a funeral home on weekend duty, once cooked for a waffle stand all night, once delivered diapers in big soft packages still warm from the dryers which he would hold against his cold body in winter as he carried them to the porches to be delivered, once ironed shirts at Lee-Ming's Progressive Chinese Hand Laundry. He talked easily of himself, and did not ask too many questions about me.

On a stair landing I glimpsed a tall girl in a navy blue dress. At second glance she was me, mirrored truly, wise-eyed and sophisticated. But Bob saw my delight and laughed at me, and for an instant I was a child again. Every now and then sunlight filtered in windows as thin as yellow smoke, and I was recalled to the day, morning, late summer, the world. There were huge cases with life-sized Indians, buffaloes, even tepees, and my own ghostly face in the glass. My voice sounded far away to me, distorted, when I laughed.

It was nearly impossible to choose what direction to go, but

Bob kept up with me and he pointed out what I had missed and with laughter that rang in my ears, said, "Frances, look at this." And I was suddenly stopped again, hushed, to hear the odd name, noted the swirling dust bits in the shaft of pale sunlight coming from one of the windows and discovered I was out of breath but still full of energy and power, so I smiled when I saw him looking at me and we looked then at headless women in fancy yellowed old-fashioned dresses— one, I think, for every president's wife.

"I used to draw paper dolls with dresses like this," I said, thinking, How long ago? Only three months? No—years and years!

The sun was bright now behind Bob's head, and his laughter reminded me of something I once read.

"What are you thinking about?" The sun halo made my eyes water and sting. Then I remembered.

"He was born with the gift of laughter and a sense that the world was mad." He shook his head, his eyes glinting, and his face was struck and pleased and so open I had to look away. "I just remembered that," I explained, "it's what you remind me of when you laugh." He only stared at me. "It's from *Scaramouche*. You know." I was sure that he did. In a second or two he nodded.

"I know," he said. Then something I decided last night came into my mind. I discovered it was easy to say, after all.

"I have to tell you something," I said. I could not escape from his eyes, bright, bright, the blue of sky or mountains or deep water. "I'm happy. I just wanted to say that. I don't think I've ever been happy before." When he didn't answer, only stared at me, I feared I had said something wrong. I didn't know what else to say, so I dropped my stinging eyes from his. His face looked worried. Puzzled by something. I shouldn't have said it.

120

"Frances?" It was like a question. I waited, still looking down, but he didn't finish. I was gradually aware of silence all around, and the soft, musty smell of all the dead things. Suddenly I wanted to leave, and my head throbbed with pain.

"What time is it?" I asked. He pushed up the sleeve of the jacket and looked at the watch on his wrist where the tiny gold wires grew.

"Ten twenty." An alarm went off in my brain and, too late, I clasped a hand to my mouth.

"Oh, no! I've missed my bus again!" He stared at me. "I'm going to Baltimore," I explained. He looked very concerned.

"Right now?" he asked, so forlorn I was delighted and had to laugh. I nodded.

"But I've missed it. It leaves now. I really have to get to Baltimore!" He still stared, seeming to think.

Then, "I could drive you," he said.

"But I couldn't pay you. I have a ticket for the bus."

"It's okay. These days don't come very often. Come on, child of light." And it was that simple.

Outside the sun screamed into my eyes, and I had to close them, swimming, against the white light. There were many cars now, and scores, maybe hundreds, of school buses in the street, all orange-yellow, all the same. We had to walk in and out among them and the honking cars until we found the cab. All sorts of wagons and booths stood around from which things to eat were sold, but he didn't suggest eating anything, so I didn't bring it up, though I was hungry again.

He called on his taxi radio that he was going to Baltimore. So I sat up front now and we edged out into the traffic. The sunlight sprinkled down on us, and the meter of the taxi was silent. As we wound snakey in and out of the slick lines of cars, he suddenly asked, "Don't you have a suitcase?" I shook my head. "Then you're not staying in Baltimore long?"

"I . . . guess not. I don't exactly know how long." And I picked at the tinfoil on the package of Life Savers I had bought at the bus station (and saved for three whole hours!), found the waxed red string, and pulled. The first one appeared, lime. Could I tell Bob about Toby Bright? The traffic was thicker than I had ever seen it. We were stopped now between two lines of cars that were going in the same direction we were, creeping along slowly. "Leeches sold here," read a sign in a drugstore window.

"Do they really sell leeches?"

"Yeah, greatest thing there is for a black eye."

"Did you ever have a black eye?"

"Yeah, once." I felt new respect for him. I was going to ask him about it but he interrupted my thoughts.

"Where does your grandmother live?"

"In Baltimore. Well—I—she'll pick me up and take me to her house." He seemed satisfied with that.

"Haven't you ever visited her before?"

"Well, no." The questions were making me very nervous. I fumbled for another Life Saver, pale as the sunlight this morning. Pineapple.

"Must not be staying long, with no suitcase." I caught the quality of his voice, quiet, controlled, and quickly got another Life Saver, red.

"I wish we could just fly up over the top of all these cars," I said, suddenly feeling closed in.

It was a desperate attempt to change the subject because I already knew what he was thinking. In the next few seconds, as he was looking at me, I felt my body grow tight as a rubber band.

"Frances, have you run away?" I swallowed hard. We were at a dead standstill now, and though I was staring straight ahead I felt him looking at me. Suddenly I grabbed his arm.

"I have to see Toby Bright!" He was looking straight into my eyes now and I said it again, clearly, not flinching from his blue, blue eyes. "I have to see Toby Bright."

"Who is that?" So, carefully, I told him about Toby Bright. He listened without comment to my story, looking at me every few seconds to nod. I even told him about how the woman on the bus wanted to save me. He relaxed somewhat, but still looked worried.

"Are you saved?" I asked him.

"Not a chance," he replied.

"What are you? I mean, like Presbyterian, or Episcopalian."

"None of those," he said, "I guess I'm not much of anything."

"Really?"

"Well, I just figure I won't waste my life getting ready for life, if you know what I mean."

I had never heard of such a thing.

"I thought everybody was something!"

He smiled. "Tell you what. You can be my Christ. I've never had a Christ before."

"But you can't *do* that," I protested, shocked.

"Why not?" he asked. I could not answer, since I knew too that Jesus was or was not, whatever each person chose to make Him. Frances's Jesus had never been the same as mine. Instead I went on to tell him about Toby Bright, the pledge, my failure just at the end, and about my sadness lately with Frances . . .

"Another Frances?" he asked.

"Yes," I said after an instant's panic, "she just happens to have the same name."

Even about Dorothy. I tried to be fair about Dorothy in the telling. I told him about everything but the kiss.

"Where does Toby Bright live?" he asked.

"In Baltimore," I said. "That's why . . ."

"Yeah, I got that part figured out a long time ago. I mean, what street?"

"I don't know." I hadn't even thought of this. Bob looked at me, then shook his head.

"Man," he said, "this just might be the craziest goddamn thing I ever did. I hope to hell we don't have a wreck." I felt very grown-up that he would say these words where I was.

"I hope not too," I said, but he only looked sideways at me and rolled his eyes.

"Where do you live?" I asked him.

"Apartment."

"Oh," I said. "Can I see it?" He looked at me, wrinkled his forehead, and widened his eyes.

"Jesus! You country girls grow up slow, don't you? I better take you back to the Greyhound where I found you."

"Oh, no, please. Don't do that! I have to get to Baltimore, Bob. Please don't leave me!" He sighed deeply, then ran his hand through his hair. He grinned a sort of sad grin.

"I don't know where I'd go," he replied, "I've got the sunshine right here. Are you hungry?" I discovered that I was—very. "We'll find someplace to eat on the way to Baltimore." He squinted his eyes up. "Look in the glove compartment and see if you can find some sunglasses."

It was full of junk: a flashlight, some leather gloves, four books, a notebook, some letters, some keys, a box of fishing hooks and little beautiful fish like jewels. I took out a double handful of things and one of the books fell into my lap. There were no sunglasses anywhere. I put everything back but the book in my lap. It was called *The Unquiet Grave*. I opened it and my eye caught a part marked with heavy red pencil:

A stone lies in a river; a piece of wood is jammed against it; dead leaves, drifting logs and branches caked with mud collect around; weeds settle and soon birds have made a nest and are feeding their young among the blossoming water plants. Then the river rises and the earth is washed away. The birds migrate, the flowers wither, the branches are dislodged and drift downward; no trace is left of the floating island but a stone submerged by the water;—such is our personality.

Many passages were marked; I had forgotten about the sunglasses. The book was like a journal, and many things about love, about writers, about some things called lemurs, were marked.

"Did you mark this?" Bob nodded, steering the cab. It was like finding someone's diary, and I had never seen a book like it before. "I could spend a month just reading this."

"You can have it if you like."

"Can I really?" He nodded.

"Sure. It's worn out anyway. I've read most of the words right off the pages. And changed the rest." And his blue eyes crumpled up with kindness that nearly drowned me. The inside of the cab, or he, I could not tell which, had a smell beautifully comfortable, comforting, that made me want to lean closer, to touch him: a musty grayish odor of rain, soap, stone cellars, cigarettes, toast. All those things and some others.

"You know," he began seriously, "it's not going to be the easiest thing, finding this Toby Bright. Baltimore is a big city. Anyhow, if you want to know what I think, I think what you're really looking for is Frances Wilson."

I experienced another of those shock-hot-cold instants when I could not remember where I was, who I was, what

time of day it was—what I was really looking for was Frances?
—me? I squeezed my eyes closed to clear my head of the
wavering light, and my eyes burnt so that tears came oozing
through the tight slits. What I really want, I thought, is this,
just this, always. But there was one change I must make, and
I was very much afraid as I forced myself to swallow and say,
"I'm not Frances Wilson; I'm Jessie Preston." I waited, looking straight ahead at the road. Incredibly, he did not hear me,
and in my relief I could not say it again. I kept the book in
my hand, glancing down at it every few seconds, feeling it a
treasure beyond value. I read Bob the part about personality,
and asked him why he marked it. After a moment, he smiled.

"Well, for instance, take today. After you're gone, I'll just
be the stone again." I thought I understood. The same, yet not
the same. Like my knowing Frances, and Dorothy. After they
are all gone I will still be—Jessie.

"Look!" I said, pointing to a sign that said "THE BLUE
NOTE! Buster resents Antonio at the Piano!" He told me then
about the menu in his favorite restaurant that read, "Dreaded
Veal Cutlets." So I told him about the congeal salad sign. I
had to be Frances just a little longer; Frances Wilson, elegant
and perfumed, poised, easy at talking to boys, and I dreaded
the time when I must again be Jessie, gawky, dirty-footed,
stupid.

Bob decided on a restaurant called Hawaiian Paradise.

"This okay?" he asked. "You can have your Hawaiian rare,
medium, or well done." I concealed the fact that I had never
been in a restaurant fancier than a bus station before.

"I don't know. This looks expensive, and I don't have very
much money."

"That's all right. I'm independently wealthy," he said.

"I'll pay you back someday when I'm rich."

"It's a deal," he grinned, and put his hand on my back to guide me through the door. I could feel the flesh burn, and all through lunch I kept remembering the pressure of his hand, just above my waist.

"We'd like a table, the countess and I," he told the fat hostess. "Near the orchestra." Countesses were married to counts! The hostess looked sour and motioned us to a small table. I felt I might pitch from my tightrope at any instant, must balance carefully so as not to fall. No one else was in the dark restaurant, and I felt just the slightest stab of disappointment to discover that the orchids on all the tables were plastic. There was a frying smell in the air, and a radio was playing the news report.

"Here we are," he said, "right in front of the orchestra," and he pulled out a chair from the tiny table set for two against the wall. "Shall I request a song?"

"Wildwood Flower," I said, "please." The waitress arrived, stringy-looking and bored, frowning.

"The countess here would like the orchestra to play Wildwood Flower," he said very importantly.

"Ain't no orchestra here," she said, "not even at night. You wanna minyew?" After she was gone, we laughed softly.

"I've never had so much fun as right now," I told Bob, "really never." This time it was he who avoided my eyes. Then I was sorry to have said it, for he looked very sad. In the quiet that followed the radio said the temperature was holding at seventy-nine degrees. To break the silence mostly, I said, "I have to go to the bathroom. I'll be back." He nodded, getting up as I did to help pull my chair back.

In the mirror I saw that I looked pretty awful, so I did some repair work on my makeup and pushed at my hair the way Lilly Anne said to. Somehow this time I didn't look as nice, even though I used the eyebrow pencil, lipstick, and powder. My dress was very wrinkled, and my eyes were rimmed with red, and the skin underneath them was a smudgy gray that even the powder wouldn't cover. *The Unquiet Grave* lay safe in my pocketbook, with all the little things I had bought. At last I went back, feeling suddenly very tired, as though all my limbs were going limp along with my dress and hair. The radio was playing a dance song now and there were two hamburgers on the table, and milk for me, coffee for Bob. He had watched me all the way across the room. As I got to the table he rose unsmiling, and pulled out my chair.

Pushing the chair in, he said, "Welcome back, Jessie." I had begun to sit; I stiffened and turned to stare at him. "Shall we laugh? Cry? Make funny faces? Or what?" He was angry.

"I tried to tell you," I said. "I *did* tell you." But he didn't believe me. "How could . . .?"

"The radio," he said, jerking his head in its direction, not taking his eyes off me. "They got one other thing wrong, though. They said you were only thirteen." I looked down, unable to think of anything else to say. "Just how much of the rest of it is lies?" he demanded. "Do you have any idea what they do to men who transport runaway little girls across state lines?" The "little girl" stabbed me in some vital area, hurt most of all.

"Just that part," I said into my lap. "All the rest is true. About Frances and Toby Bright and Dorothy. Honestly," I said, but the blue eyes were a solid wall, hard as diamonds in this murky place.

"I ought to leave you right here, and get the hell back to Washington where it's safe. Nothing but drunks and murderers." But even in his saying this was the promise that he wouldn't.

"Please don't," I said. "You have to help me."

"Do I? Why?"

"Because you're the only friend I have."

"Friend, Jessie?" he asked, narrowing his eyes. "I should have guessed you were only thirteen. Don't you know *why* men take girls to museums?" I shook my head. "Do you think it is reasonable to expect you'll be safe with some—cab driver? How do you know I'm not some maniac who's going to carry you off to the woods and rape and murder you?" But I was not fooled or frightened.

"You're a gentleman," I said. I watched him visibly relax and light a cigarette.

"I guess there's just no answer for that," he said. "Your faith is well misplaced, I suppose." And he blew out pale, pearly smoke that wound upward like a ribbon.

"Could I please have a cup of coffee?" I asked. He nodded, called the waitress over.

"How do you want it?" I had to think fast.

"Black," I said. He nodded to the waitress.

"Make it two—one black, one sugar." This milestone would apparently be passed without comment. He didn't say anything to me, just sat smoking and staring into space, until the waitress came.

"Okay," he said, when the coffee was before us, in a tone of voice to indicate that everything had been settled. He took a deep breath. "I'm a gentleman. And gentlemen take care of little runaway girls. And now I have to help the helpless princess escape her undoubtedly frantic, wicked stepmother, to find some boy, some prince, aged—what, *fourteen?*—who you say is ugly, who lives somewhere in Baltimore, the seventh goddamn largest city in the United States. For what, Jessie? Do you think you can just go and live with him? Are you going to marry him? Do you think people just do what they want all the time? Drink your coffee and stop staring. And finally, do you think you can just go around picking up strange men to carry you on adventures to see other men?" He was only part angry, and I was not sure what to say. His anger was nothing like Dorothy's, and I knew that throughout it all he still liked me.

"I didn't just pick you up, you picked *me* up; and I didn't ask you to take me to Baltimore, either," I said.

"But you lied about your age, even your name. For Crissakes, *why* did you lie about your *name*?" I wanted to say, Because Jessie Preston does everything wrong, ruins everything, and I want to be someone else. But it didn't make any sense. After the nest and birds are gone, the stone is still the same.

So I just said, "I'm terribly sorry."

"And what about Toby Bright?" His voice was slower now, not urgent anymore. But he was relentless. "What's he going to do when you show up? Hide you in his snake cage? What if he has another girlfriend by now? Grow up, Jessie, and stop your dreaming." His voice was quiet now. "Look. I'm going to put you on the nearest bus for wherever it is you live." And suddenly the thought of the loss of him was too great to bear, yet, now. I reached across and put my hand on his hand.

"Bob. Please, you have to help me. You're the only person who can help me now."

"No, Jessie Preston. *You're* the only person who can help you now." Somewhere between the two statements the truth lay. I knew at that moment that Toby Bright was only one-tenth real. He had written me no letters, was merely being kind, kissed me only to stop my crying, was only a boy.

"Would you stay just a little longer?" I asked him, very

quietly, holding my breath against forever. He dropped his eyes.

"Ah, Jessie." He put his head into his hands, elbows on the table, and said my name with finality, though even to hear him say it was warming, was relieving, for the mask was now truly gone. For what had I gone barefoot all summer? I could never escape being Jessie. The stone. His blue eyes stared into mine for many seconds. "The makeup isn't necessary," he said. "Why don't you go wash your face?"

"I think," I said, "that I'd like to go home." For I had had today, and it was real, and if jail was the price, then I was ready to pay it. I didn't know whether they put you in jail for running away. Maybe if I got put in jail, at least I could talk to Mr. Ever Summer. We could sing hillbilly songs together. It might not be so bad after all.

"Borden," he said. "The radio said Borden. Where the hell is that?" So I told him the bigger places near it, and he nodded. "Okay," he said, finally, "I'll take you." I let out my breath. The world was solid and would hold, at least a while longer.

"One more thing," I said. "About what you said. Were you really a count?"

"A *count*?" He wrinkled his forehead. "What in the world are you talking about?"

6

Rose sounded the same. I might have been calling from Dorothy's. Bob waited outside the ovenish telephone booth, rubbing the back of his neck slowly. Sun glinted off his hair. Even in the glare of afternoon he kept on his windbreaker of bronzy gray; he was a picture of gold and silver, his back to me, a passing car causing a ruffling, a slight billowing, against the whiteness of the air while Rose's voice and mine traveled eerily back and forth in a long blue tube, the things we both had to say. In the distance a sign said in red letters: "37 Miles to Fort Hell—Ice Cream." All in all, I didn't think she sounded very mad.

"They didn't even call the police until eleven. They thought I was in the woods. First they just thought I had slept late." He smiled.

"What did you tell them . . ." he slanted his eyes around

and arched his eyebrow, whiter than his skin, "regarding your mode of transportation home?"

"I told her you were very nice—a gentleman—and pretty old."

"Oh, *very* old," he concurred.

"How old?"

"Ancient."

"How old *really*?"

"Thirty-three."

"That's how old my father was."

"When?"

"He was always thirty-three. I mean, that's when he died. You're supposed to drive carefully," I informed him, frowning at the speedometer.

"Do you remember your father?"

"No. He killed himself. Drinking. He was common."

"Who told you *that*?"

"Dorothy. William Devine was his name. Preston is my mother's name. She died when I was born, and Dorothy took me because my father wasn't fit to have me."

"Does everyone think that your father was common?"

"I guess so. Except maybe Willa."

"Willa?"

"She's my grandmother. She came to Dorothy's funeral. I think she is my father's mother."

"You *think* so?" I was confused by this conversation. "Where does she live?"

"Willa? In Borden."

"Do you go to see her very much?" I was surprised.

"No. I've never been to see her." Bob stared at me a long instant.

"Don't you think that's a pretty lopsided view?" I thought

about it, but before I could answer he asked, "Would you like to give old Toby Bright a call, now you're in the area, just for old times' sake?"

"No, I don't think so." What, oh, what, of Toby Bright now? I felt confused, seemed then to have somehow ruined the future already in my dreams; but I wouldn't call him; as long as it all never really happened, I guessed, it could never change, and I saw that nothing that he could say in a phone call could ever be as wonderful as what I had dreamed. What I would do was write it all up in my autobiography: before my eyes a book cover (red) arose: *Gone with the Summer*, by Jessie Preston, Famous Author of *Gone with the Summer*. I remembered they did that on covers.

On the trip back through Washington, the cab got hotter and hotter and I kept closing my eyes and trying to understand what was happening. I felt strange, almost lightheaded, and time was a changeable thing. I kept forgetting when it was; I would open my eyes and everything would be silver-edged. Now I would not ever call Toby Bright or go to Baltimore to live with him, and beneath their lids my eyes watered; what would happen to me when I went back? If the dream of Toby Bright wasn't real, then what was? The bleak beginning of school again in two weeks stretched before me; I longed to be over it all, to be grown up, beyond this confusion and pain. *Toby Bright, when will we, never, never in the month of June, horses neighing in German, the weight of honeysuckle heavy as a quilt. Oh, never, never, never by cool Siloam's shady rill with all the world's kisses waiting, never.* I looked up to see Bob Brunelli beside me, real and quiet, but I had ruined even that. He was looking at the road, his eyes wrinkled at the corners in concentration.

My life was running out, and I was only thirteen. It had

always been like that; I was always behind in my life. I hadn't learned how to be a charming little girl until I was too old to act like one. Finally, I had gotten that mastered, only to have Dorothy say to Rose, when she thought I wasn't listening," . . . Like a child. For heaven's sakes, she's eleven years old!" I felt I could face Toby Bright now without horror, could apologize, even, for being so foolish. But what need? He had not written, had probably forgotten my name in the long months that stretched back to his visit. And what could I say now to Bob? Whatever it was, I wasn't ready for it. Could I ever hope to be a good wife, a smart mother, until some distant lavender winter day when I was old and alone, and would know everything, and it would all be too late?

"I have to go to the bathroom," I said.

I could lock myself in here, in the deodorized coolness, and never go out again, never have to go to the eighth grade, to live all those dreary days. Someday would come a silent summer when no birds would sing that I could hear, and I would be what the stones were now. I felt as tired as if I had lived a thousand years, would have lain down on the cold tile in all this green and white, eyes pressed against the white side of the washbasin, would have imagined it a bed where I would sleep forever, an iceberg that would float endlessly and gently in green water. When I closed my eyes I could still see the white lines on the road, running out like my life.

But I went back, and he was smoking a cigarette and waiting, and that he looked glad to see me nearly broke my heart.

"It's this sun," I explained, "it really hurts your eyes, doesn't it?"

"Terrible. I'll complain to the authorities. And we'll stop for supper soon." He had the kindest face I had ever seen.

The sky was turning red and the blue hills rolled up in front of us when we stopped to have supper. I hated to go inside and miss the beautiful changes.

"You seen one sunset, you seen them all, I always say," but then he winked and I knew he was kidding. He watched it for a minute. "I know it has a reason, and it's all neatly scientific, but it *looks* like someone spilled paint on the mountains and set the rim of the sun on fire."

He was so beautiful, his skin copper in the ruddy light, that I had to change the subject. "Look!" I said, "There's a dragon, and a plate of peach ice cream!"

"Well, I'll be damned. There sure is. I'll have to kill the dragon, of course. You certainly do attract them." He brandished a sword bravely. I could almost hear it swish the air.

"I'll eat the ice cream while you do it." I was Maid Marian again.

"You women are all alike," he complained, opening the door. "You could at least save me a bite." His hand did not touch my back this time, and he would not say my name. But it was an awfully nice restaurant, with blue lights reflecting in a shallow pool out front, and air-conditioned insides. He ordered a kind of French soup for us called vichyssoise.

"Mine's cold," I told him. He ducked his head. "What's so funny?" But I fared better after that, sticking with things I knew: fried shrimp, french fries, and strawberry shortcake. "Did you ever go to the Grand Ole Opry?" I asked him.

"Sure. A lot when I was a kid. Once I even took Martha." He chuckled, a wry smile on his face.

"Who's she?" I asked, though I knew the answer.

"My wife." He said it quietly, simply, sadly, looking off into some distance. I tried to see what he was looking at and could not. Looking at his face was like looking into the sun.

I hadn't wanted to say anything that might remind him of

her, but since he was already reminded, I said, "Where is she?"
He slowly blew out some blue smoke that seemed to get into
his eyes, rising in a layer like chiffon between us.

"Memphis," he said, in the saddest voice imaginable. Then
he added, as if he wasn't talking to me anymore, but to the
rose walls of the restaurant, "With her mother. And my
money. *And* my best friend, at last report." I tried to see them,
but gave up.

"Does she like hillbilly music?"

"No." Gratitude swept over me, and my eyes were cups
filled too full.

"*I* do," I said, and couldn't tell why he smiled. "Is she
pretty?" He only nodded. I sniffed.

"She's a ballet dancer." A wonder! I had planned an ordinary housewife. A ballet dancer!

"Was she—why did you get divorced?"

"We're not divorced yet. It'll be soon."

"Soon?" The bone at the base of his cheek bulged out
slightly as though inside his mouth his teeth were clenched
tight together. "Then why are you *getting* divorced?"

"Well," and again his hand rubbed the back of his neck,
"it's a long story. First she fell in love with a tenor." A
familiar word: what is it? "That's a singer." And then I remembered the one I had seen—with Frances—at a concert
last winter; she had seemed to know something about them.
I had asked her if she knew why their voices were so high.
She said she had read that they had operations to make them
that way. Is that why he's got a beard—to cover up the scar?
I think so, she had said.

"Did he have that operation?" I asked Bob. He first looked
puzzled, and then laughed.

"Boy, you really are out of a nursery rhyme! They don't

have operations—but never mind. She doesn't like him any- more anyway; she's in love with my best friend now, or at least that's what I heard last." He sighed, leaned back, and lit a cigarette.

"Are you still . . . I mean, do you still . . . ?"

"Love her?" he finished. "Yes. I think so. Probably. A fate worse than death." He smiled without happiness. "That's a line from a play." I could feel my heart begin to thump against my ribs like a bird trying to escape from its cage.

"You could maybe wait for me to get older. I wouldn't ever divorce you," I said, leaning toward him. His eyes closed tightly until nothing showed except gold eyelashes and crinkles.

"You'll be too busy running away from dragons to be thinking of getting married. There are a lot of dragons around, you know."

"I'll read lots of books. A girl in our school got married when she was fifteen. That's only two years. Of course she had a baby too soon."

"Can't have *that* happening. Think of how embarrassed the baby must have been!" He smoked the cigarette for a minute. "Jessie . . ." How could my name sound so new, so magic? "Education isn't all in books . . . and not a bit of growing up is. Dances, dates . . . you have all that ahead. Come on, child of light." He pushed back his chair.

He leaned over, and said, in a scandalized whisper, "We certainly won't come *here* anymore. Their soup's *cold*." He rolled his eyes in horror. I managed to grin weakly. He laughed and I changed the subject to something I had had on my mind.

"When we get to Borden, will you take me to the jail?" He looked surprised. "There's someone there I have to see."

"Are *many* of your friends in jail?"

So I told him about Ever Summer and he said he guessed it would be all right, grinning down at me as if I were a child. He felt first in one pocket, then in another, finally slapping at all his pockets.

"Jesus!" he said under his breath.

"Yes?" I asked, in a small voice, but he didn't notice.

"I forgot all about money. I'm broke. For lunch they clipped me for a buck six bits." The words bounced around inside my skull like some kind of music. "My present fortune amounts to thirty-six cents. No checks. What are you worth?"

"Here's three dollars and four cents." I counted it out from the dark blue cave of my pocketbook. The bird's nest was still there, but disintegrating slowly into rubble at the bottom. I found the quartz.

"We could sell this." I held it out with a twinge of sorrow.

"It's a perfect one," he said, "but I can't have you selling your jewels for me. It really is a pretty one."

"I was going to take it to Toby Bright but I'd like to give it to you. Just for a present, then, not to sell." He turned it over, looked at it.

"Okay," he said. "I'll keep it always." Then I remembered how I could help us.

"Bob! I can forge things. I mean, really. I know Rose's handwriting exactly. I could . . ."

"You could *what*? Get us put in jail, that's what! There we'd be: you and Ever Summer and I . . . terrific." He set his jaw, looked hard at me. I hung my head.

"I'm probably going to jail anyway, after today."

"Probably," he agreed, hands on hips like Rose. "On the other hand, I expect it's been a week or two since they put a kid in jail just for running away. But forgery is another matter entirely. Don't you realize that the only person you can *be* is Jessie? Not other people . . . not other people's names . . . not even other people's writing."

"Okay," I said, very low. "Then I'll wash."

"You'll what?"

"Wash. The dishes. You're laughing *again*. What's so funny?" And I began, for the second time that day, some odd combination of laughing and crying. But it turned out all right, because instead of Kleenex, I came up with two more dollars.

Bob came back with change, which he dropped into my hand. We pushed the glass door outward into the warm purple night.

"Good thing we've got plenty of gas," he said. "All day I've felt like a minor character in a major tragedy, but I'm beginning to decide it's a comedy after all."

Jewels in the darkness; eyes of *yes* and *no* flared in bunches or singly as we slowed to pass through towns; stop, go again, the air new with pine and night and gasoline and smoke and leather. Once it skimmed my mind that we were going backward to get to the future, by dark, by yellow light, by chilled lavender air, by white road markings one by one. Whatever I had thought was not so. I had been wrong about nearly everything. The motor settled to a quiet rumbling that shook me limp in the dark lap of leather; the rising hills rounded the swinging corners of flat half dreams and swelled to vaulted, plunging silence that was rushing music and dark red.

"Jessie. Wake up." And I swam upward through thinning layers of sleep like lapping water, trying to see through burnt eyelids, lifting my head with difficulty from the warm starch-smelling roughness of his lap. "This seems to be Borden," Bob said out of the darkness. Could we be there already? It was all about to end, and time like sand ran out through the helpless errors of my hands.

There might still be a reprieve, if only a temporary one.

"The jail," I managed to say, my heart failing, it seemed so late. "Can we still go to the jail?"

The night policeman had been asleep; that was obvious. One side of his face had the lines of a pillow on it, and he kept tasting his mouth as if there were something in it that he didn't like. Bob explained what we wanted. The policeman ran his fingers comblike through his hair.

"Bastard's prolly asleep," he commented, leading us down a hall. "Hickman!" he yelled.

The man in wine gabardine slacks and a pale green shirt jumped, roused himself. "What in hell . . . ?"

"Watch yer language. It's a lay-dee!" He turned to me with an exaggerated bow. "Lady, I 'pologize for this *gentleman*. He don't know his back end from a hole in the ground." Then grinning at Ever Summer, more ordinary, slighter, than I had imagined, "It's yer fan club. They wanna *talk* to you." He chuckled, scratched his stomach.

"Mr. Summer, this is Jessie Preston, an admirer of yours," Bob said cautiously.

"Yeah?" he asked. I could not think of one thing to say, so I nodded vigorously. The officer clanked back to the front, leaving us standing before the barred room.

"Mr. Summer," I began, "I know you like hillbilly music." My mouth was dry.

"Yeah," he said.

"Well, I want to say that—I think you're very brave."

"You from the newspaper?" he said to Bob.

141

"No, sir," Bob said. "I'm just escorting Miss Preston here."

"No kidding," he said, looking from Bob to me and back again. "No kidding." And the second time he sounded impressed.

"Mr. Summer, I hope you get out of jail real soon," I said. "I read about you in the paper." He didn't say anything. "Mr. Summer, could you play something on your guitar?" I looked for the sparkling suit but in all the stone room there was only one peg, and on it was a thin rayon striped coat in two colors of brown.

"I ain't got no guitar no more."

"You don't?" He reached his hand up and ran it through his hair, thin and oily, and rolled his eyes up at the ceiling.

"Nope. Reckon it was too loud for 'em. Then again, I was just learning."

"What happened to the purple car?" I asked. Bob was rubbing the back of his neck again, and I could tell he wanted to go. Ever Summer shrugged.

"What the hell you want anyway?" he demanded listlessly. "I'm tard." He yawned to prove it, and I noticed his teeth were very bad. Then he came close to the bars. "You ain't got no Dr. Peppers, do you?"

"Not a one," Bob said, moving in close. "Sorry, pal."

"I could maybe bring you some," I said.

"I could maybe use some, I reckon." He was eyeing me very closely the whole time. "Uh, who'd you say you was?"

I opened my mouth to answer but Bob said with exaggerated pleasantness, "She's not available, pal," and put his arm around my shoulder, smiling at Ever Summer.

"I could still bring him some Dr. Peppers," I said.

"That'll be okay, as long as that's *all*," Bob said. Mr. Summer backed away from the bars, and put his hands, palms out, in front of his face.

"Okay, mac."

"Jess," Bob said, "let's blow this joint."

"Goodbye, Mr. Summer. I'll bring you . . ." but Bob nearly jerked my arm out of my armhole, causing me to lose balance and fall against him. Bob had called me a new name: Jess: I liked it.

"Good luck, pal," Bob said over his shoulder to Ever Summer as he pulled me roughly down the corridor back to the police office. I felt annoyed at being mishandled.

"What're you *doing*?" He didn't stop, just made his mouth into a smile that left his eyes out altogether, while I resisted, as much as anything else, the moment that was nearly upon us. The huge clock just over the door said ten forty-five. I had never been out anywhere that late, and especially with a boy (which I at once changed to "man"), and *especially* one who was, as far as I could see, jealous. In fact, I broke into song: "I ree-mem-BURR the night . . ." but he interrupted.

"Come on, Veronica Lake, let's go," he said. "That's my state song you're desecrating." He practically shoved me into the cab. "If I start playing the guitar, you'll know I'm jealous." In the darkness I grinned to myself: MISS JESSIE PRESTON WINS BEAUTY CONTEST.

They were all on the front porch. Around the light, moths and beetles banged and buzzed. I performed the introductions; Charlie nodded and grunted welcome while Rose thanked Bob for such a kindness, and I noticed that Frances didn't quite know what to do. She looked sweaty and was barefoot and awkward. Rose could talk to anyone, and I was grateful to her for the first time.

"I know you're tired. Won't you stay overnight with us?" Could it possibly have been only one day since I was standing here, in this very spot? Would he stay?

"Please!" I said.

"No, thank you; I'll have to go right back. But I found Jessie, and it just seemed to me I had to see her safely home. Besides," he wrinkled his brow, "a beautiful creature like Jessie isn't safe traveling alone! I had to slay at least one dragon on the way here—or was it two?" Charlie chuckled, Rose laughed, and Frances just sat with her mouth hanging slightly open.

"At least you'll have a cup of coffee before you go back, won't you?" He said he'd like that.

"After all, I've had to put up with Jessie since about seven thirty this morning." I couldn't contain myself.

"We spent all morning at the Smithsonian! You know, Frances, the place Toby Bright told us about!" Frances merely nodded, staring at me; her eyes reminded me of chocolate-covered cherries. It was the first time I had come out like that in public and said his name. The spell was broken.

The green kitchen felt like home for once. We all sat around the table, drinking coffee, though Rose poured more milk in Frances's and mine than I felt was necessary. Bob told them all the right details, none of the wrong ones, and I told about the bus ride. Frances was fidgety and hardly said a thing. But our round table was short-lived, for in only fifteen minutes he stood up to leave.

"How much do we owe you, Mr. er—?" Charlie asked, reaching for his wallet.

"Not a thing, Mr. Wilson. It was one of the nicest days I've ever spent." I tried to memorize his face and voice and size and colors. "Besides," he added, "Jessie had to pay for our dinner." The flash of his smile, the last, for me alone.

In the moment of confusion that always accompanies good-byes, Charlie pulled me aside and shoved a crumpled bill into

my hand. I knew what it was for and said, "Thanks, Charlie."
We grinned at each other, and in a flash of revelation I saw
that here was a friend, and that Charlie was glad I had come
home.

I walked with Bob, or rather, ran behind him down the
driveway, he walked so fast.

"Bob, Bob . . ."

"Yes?" I wanted to remember everything, every word.

"Bob, you have to take this. Charlie wants you to."

"No," he said. "I—" but then he seemed to change his mind
abruptly. "Fine," he said. "Thank him for me, Jessie." And
he took it without looking and shoved it into his hip pocket.

"Bob—?" It was dark all around us, we were out of earshot
and out of the porch light's reach. "Bob—" Maybe if I stood
closer to him—he was waiting, though, his hand on the door
of the taxi, so odd in our driveway. "Bob, I just can't think
what I want to say—"

"You don't always have to use words to talk," he said. "I'm
going now. Thanks for a lovely day, Jessie."

"No—wait—" But what could I say, here, in the darkness,
the smell so tentative it was almost not a smell, of dampness
on grass, of night itself, of the leather, the cigarettes, the
starch?—I stared beyond his head at the jeans-blue sky.
"Couldn't you maybe—kissmegoodbye?"

An eon of silence passed. I stood as close as I dared. Then
came the faintest, smallest touch on the top of my head. I
waited, eyes closed, the night sky whirling about my head,
but that was all. *Here, quickly, before I fall beyond this falling day where everything changes forever—*

"Jess, it's been a long day. Go on in, now." His hand
touched my shoulder, pushed me away from him, toward the
Wilsons.

"Will you write to me?"

"Maybe."

"Promise?"

"No promises. I'm old enough to be your father." He seemed to be talking not to me, not to anyone, yet his words so stunned me for an instant I could not hear what else he was saying. "The best things of all aren't permanent. Remember the stone in the river?"

"Yes, I'll read the whole book, every word. I'll read lots of books! I'll write to you."

"Just live. Have some more days like today. When Toby Bright comes again you'll have today to tell him about. You were a princess today."

"Won't you ever come back?"

"Probably not. It might ruin today."

"It's not fair!" I said, trying to keep my voice from wobbling, to him, to Toby Bright, to the stars that spun and aged around my head.

"Sure it is. All's fair that ends happily. But don't go running off anymore."

There were still the bright words, the amazing words I had just last night planned to say to someone else; all had changed in a day and I could not be untruthful. I love you; I love you, I said inside, but no words came out.

He must have known, for he said, "Don't be so unhappy. You'll love lots of people."

"No," I said, "nobody else," half hoping that he would misunderstand, that he would think I meant Toby Bright. When he spoke again his voice sounded almost harsh.

"It'll be midnight soon and you know what happens at midnight."

"What?"

"Princesses turn into pumpkins. You better go on in."

"Please don't go!" But he did; he got in the car and he drove off and he didn't look back once. But before he had gone, I had reached in the window to him, had touched his head in the dark, and felt I would never forget in all my life the feel of his hair on my hand.

That night I slept a million years, clinging to Brown Sugar, my only anchor on a desolate sea.

7

Summer, bottle-green, wound slowly down to mellow, yellow fall. At school I wasn't the tallest anymore. In fact, Bobby Lowenstein was lots taller. He also was good at algebra, which I didn't understand for two hoots.

"What did you ever do with the alligator?" I asked him one day on the way out of algebra.

"You mean old Jessie?"

"*Jessie?*"

"Sure," he said, "I named her after you. But I'm not really sure it was a girl."

"That's okay. How come you named it Jessie?"

"I just did. After you. I took her to camp. That's why I had to get rid of her. I was going to camp."

"What happened?"

"I tried to trade her off to everybody there too. She kept

growing, and ate too much. I brought her leftover peanut butter and jelly sandwiches every night."

"Weren't they bad for her?"

"I think so. One day she just up and died. I don't think she really *liked* peanut butter all that much. We had a funeral and put up a tombstone. 'Jessie' we wrote on it. The whole camp went. She was a great alligator." He sighed. "Are you going to the homecoming dance?"

"No," I said.

"Well, would you like to?" he asked.

"You're airbrushed," Frances said, as I tore back the flap on the letter. It was our night to cook dinner for our home ec. homework. We both had mail, she an advertisement for some other kind of Wate-On pills than the ones she'd already ordered and was taking by the hundreds (she still couldn't swallow pills without water very well), and the class pictures we'd had taken for the annual; I had a letter, glistening white: how had I never noticed the beautiful proportions of a legal envelope, the handwriting unmistakably the same as that which was on the margins of the Book, nearly as good as his presence whenever I opened it?

"You look pretty anyway," she said, "you look better than I do." I barely looked. The yellow hair waved at me.

"Frances! He wrote to me!" I couldn't seem to catch my breath. Out fell a clipping from a newspaper, jackknifing its way to the floor and flipping over on its back. It was from a Washington paper: he had written the date at the top: it read: "For Sale, one Cadillac, pastel purple, convertible, road-tested; one sequined suit, green, sz. 32; one electric guitar with amplifier, Hawaiian. All three or separate, if interested call collect 596, Borden, Virginia. William Tolliver Tinseley

Real Estate." For some reason I felt pride as I read it. It was like a part of me. But the letter itself warmed my lap alive as an animal, and I undid its triple folds with hands that suddenly felt paralyzed, felt like heavy gross tools for some delicate task.

"Dear Jessie," it began, "I cut this out weeks ago and meant to send it to you, but it was right before I left and it got stuck in a book somewhere. Only today I came across it." He had left Washington, was back in Memphis and back with Martha. Things were different, he said. He had begun to write again, he wanted to know if I had read *The Unquiet Grave* (yes, beautiful, like finding treasures every time, but what did they mean?). And last of all—

"Frances! You'll never guess—look—" and I showed where he'd written, "Would you like to come to see us for part of your Christmas vacation? Martha and I would both like that. For a seasoned bus rider like you it wouldn't be a long trip."

"Frances! I couldn't! It would be—well, awful!" Her turn to stare.

"Why?"

I couldn't really answer, but I was certain that I could never go: where he was would be too much magic. There would be: the ballet dancer; me. I would be terrible. What would I do but sit? And she?—she would dance around the house in a rose-colored tutu. I just couldn't. I scanned the letter again and again for some trace of love, some word that would recall our day, our part of the story, the part without the ballet dancer. There was only one reminder, at the end: "Seen any good dragons lately?" It made me laugh out loud, and I spun around on the kitchen floor making a dizziness of the room, red, gree-ee-een, that whirled around me echoing with the laugh. I felt wonderful, and carefully I replaced the beautiful letter and began to bread the pork chops. Frances said, slicing the cabbage, that Phillips Hepwaite had asked her to the homecoming dance.

There was one thing for sure I owed Bob, and me. So Saturday afternoon, my hair clean for the dance at eight, I went to see Willa.

The house looked deserted. Dust lay on the carved wood of the porch railings and on the peeling, rotting floor. The only porch furniture was an iron table and two iron chairs, also dirty. I twisted the doorbell and heard it ring within, and echo deeply, as though the house were empty of rugs and furniture. It was afternoon, but it looked like night in that house. I juggled the carton of Dr. Peppers to the other arm, wishing I could have left it somewhere. Rose had let me off at the grocery corner, and I had two hours for my errands. The October day was brisker than I had thought. Two dirty children stood on the sidewalk and watched me with big eyes. I shivered slightly, and hunched closer into my sweater.

"You goin' in there?"

"Yes."

"You know Miz Devine?" I nodded.

"She's a pret' nice lady," the other child said. They bobbed their heads up and down at that. "Give us a cookie yestiddy."

I decided she wasn't there.

"Maybe she'll give us one *today*." They grinned at each other. Finally, the boy nudged the girl, and they skipped off down the street. The little girl's thin voice rose in a song, the little boy's voice joining in to make a high crazy duet:

"I love coffee, I love tea,
I love the boys and the boys love me!

First comes love, then comes marriage,
Then comes Suzie with a bay-bee carriage!"

She wasn't coming. I turned to leave, and heard a sound in-side, as Willa unlocked the door.

"I've come to ask you about my father." I hadn't meant to be blunt, but there we were, sitting across from each other in a room that might once have been beautiful, but now was drab, sparse, dark brown, dark red, decorated with only two wall pictures and ugly sparse furniture. Up high against the ceiling were elegantly carved white moldings, the carvings deepened and accented with dust. My heart pushed upward at my throat, and I found it hard to breathe. The pictures were a cross-stitched faded sampler that read: "Christ is the Head of This House, and He is the Master Within," and a dark rich painting of Jesus ascending to heaven and giving a benedic-tion to all those on earth. On a table underneath were two small photographs in silvery frames. I tried to look at Willa but my eyes kept jumping over to the pictures of the two men.

"The near one," she said. I stared at the face until it flowed blue-white at the edges, until I had to use my star-trick to see it, until the eyes seemed to come alive. The eyes were the same as mine, I thought. And the ears were normal-sized, not small at all.

"Frances laughed at me and said everybody knew Santa Claus was dead except me. I thought Santa Claus was my father. I even asked Dorothy once if I could see a picture of my father, but she said she didn't have one." Willa adjusted her gold-rimmed glasses, petite as the rest of her.

"What did Dorothy tell you about William?"

"Only that he—" but Dorothy's bones were laid in the ground, and all education wasn't in books, and they were all dead—"that he loved my mother and was a very nice man." I swallowed, wondering if she would accept it. It sounded too easy, and very unnatural. I slicked my eyes over for an instant to see how she was reacting. She looked disbelieving; I couldn't blame her for that; and her delicate pale hands clutched like claws the claw arms of her chair.

"I never thought Dorothy Preston understood William." She spoke very slowly, her voice wavering just the tiniest bit. "It was hard to understand that she never wanted William to see you at all."

"Why didn't she?" I felt as though to ask was to enter some cave of which I knew nothing, in which I might discover treasure or death, and a drop of sweat traveled deliberately the length of my backbone like a spider on an afternoon stroll. Because: he was common; because: she had the right. The picture of him was a miracle; his hair was thick and yellow like mine, and he squinted into the camera the way I always did. There would be gold wiry hairs on the backs of his hands. Willa didn't seem to hear me.

"Eight years in a town is a long time. Time enough for everything and everyone to change. He came home just that once. Except for the second time. And never again . . ." Her voice trailed off, but then she jerked herself back. "For an exhibition of his painting."

"My father was an artist?"

"Yes, an artist. But not successful. He saw Dorothy Preston with a beautiful girl that day. He asked Dorothy who she was when Dorothy told him he'd done right well since high school, that he'd raised himself. 'My little sister,' she said, 'she's a student at the seminary. And too young for the likes of you, William Devine.' Dorothy was already an old maid then."

"He loved my mother?"

"He never even saw anyone else. Just seemed like he'd never *seen* any girl with his eyes until Virginia came along. Came home for supper talking about her dark hair and her white skin."

"Why didn't he keep me?"

"When you were born he had to bring your mother's body back here to be buried. That was the only other time he ever came home." She sighed heavily. "When I found out he had died, it was too late. And I had nobody to help me." Her eyes were seeing things I could not see.

"And he loved my mother." I could feel the anger rising up from the empty cave of my stomach, up, up, to spread its redness at the injustice upon my chest, my neck, my face. "Why didn't he love me? I was just a baby. Why did he let *her* have me?" Outside the window the white light glazed an oak tree to coppery gold, shimmery at the edges, dull brown spreading upon its leaves like sickness. Willa went on, talking to herself.

"Virginia. They both lived here, grew up here, and he never so much as saw her until that day. Dorothy Preston didn't approve of it at all." She shook her head sadly.

"But what about me?" She brought her eyes back from looking at something far off.

"You? Before he went back he would go at night and stand on the sidewalk by the Preston house and listen on his way back from the cemetery, just to see could he hear you cry. She had a colored girl for you then."

"Why didn't he take me back to New York? How could he just go off—and leave me? His own baby?"

"His own? Dorothy just took you."

"And he *let* her?" Willa narrowed her eyes and stared at me.

"He had no choice. She had the right to take you."

"But *why?*" How far had I come to hear this? In the instant before she said it, I sensed, heard, knew what I had not known before, what I had always known. Willa glanced at the picture, then down at her lap, then at me.

"Jessie? Can it be she never told you?"

"Told me what?" And I moved to the very edge of the chair.

"That Virginia and William never were married." It took me an instant to understand as though it were about two people who had nothing to do with me. Did it matter? *For permanence is not the test. The best things aren't permanent.* Bob's book said it. He had said it. Could I wish myself unborn? Willa leaned forward, still clutching the claws of the chair. "Jessie, you don't know how much he loved you. There were all kinds of reasons." Her hands left the chair and fluttered around like frightened birds. "But he gave you his beauty," and she cupped my hot face in her cool small hands and smiled, a little smile. "Would you like to have the picture?" I only nodded, could not speak. There was a lot more, but I would come back. I had to think about all this for a while.

I seemed to be walking to sleep through a pool of thin October sunshine, to the spot where we had parked the taxi, to the stone steps, to the very room with the clock, to the desk behind which sat another police officer.

"I just brought some Dr. Peppers, because I promised to. I —could you just give them to him?" I was terrified that I might have to see Mr. Ever Summer again, but a promise was a promise.

"Man, they took him to Richmond two weeks ago. He got two years. He won't be able to use them Dr. Peppers for a while, I reckon. Friend of yours?"

"Sort of," I said, and let out my breath slowly.

It was getting colder when I walked back out the heavy door carting the Dr. Peppers and my father's picture. There was still almost an hour before I had to meet Rose. I shivered in the pale light and turned off Main Street toward the cemetery, my feet picking their own way over the glazed bricks with their circles-within-squares pattern, useless for roller skating. The other man—the other picture: my grandfather? I would ask Willa. Through the thin air of afternoon the last arrows of sun seemed to rest upon the empty street. The air was ivory, clean as linen, the snap of a twig from a dead tree clear as a spark in the quiet. I neared the cemetery and suddenly a quail rose noisily, shattering the gray like a brown clod thrown into the sky. Where were his brothers and sisters? The skin of my hand looked transparently white, and I buttoned up the sweater against the chill. I knew Dorothy had said *married*. I was sure she had. Stones and crosses, gray velvet ground, quiet graves harmonious with earth and air, rose to block my way as I walked, watching the bird heavenward for a moment above the pen-sketched trees and bushes, to the stone with doves and a cross:

Virginia Preston
May 4, 1916–July 8, 1939
Rest in God

Next to it a square stone said,

Dorothy Scott Preston
January 19, 1908–June 20, 1950
With her Maker

A few brown leaves dipped and twirled downward and scraped along the stones with a paper-on-paper sound. A vague smoky smell hung in the air, reminiscent of fire and winter and times I could not really remember, like things from a dream. Slow thick ivy covered the ground here, the only green in this gray place of miracles or stone, I did not know which. In some other stone place my father lay, but that didn't matter. Silence like the end of something lay everywhere. I stood until the chill crept up my arms and legs, flesh closing upon itself, shrinking into itself. I thought that I might, after all, go to Memphis: in the distance my house, red brick, stared vacantly from empty windows. One of the window panes was broken. Already it was dying; the cemetery advanced and I understood that the house would be sold. It was all Dorothy had left me, and I had nothing else. Charlie had told me that. I could live with them as long as I wanted, but the money from the house I needed for college someday. A few yards farther between two old maples, streaked with blood-red color, stood three softened stones, their angels blurred in the twilight.

Maria Nagle White
June 5, 1889–July 14, 1909
Beloved Consort

Thomas Nagle White
July 2, 1909–July 12, 1909

Thomas White
December 5, 1888–April 4, 1950

Forty-one years he had waited! I didn't know them; how had they died? How had he endured? I sat on Maria's stone and watched the sunset streak with blood the purple sky. I picked up a Dr. Pepper, and found I could hook the top underneath the edge of the gravestone. After a minute or so, the cap came off, and I took a sip of the fuzzy drink, strangely warm in the cold of afternoon, with the flavor of prunes. It wasn't bad, but it wasn't good either. Thomas White's words alone stood out clearly, still sharp and new: "Remember man as you pass by, As you are now so once was I; As I am now you too will be, Therefore think on Eternity."

I couldn't have told how long I had sat before the murmur of voices rising to light laughter caused me to look up. They were moving slowly toward me, in a silence so complete I wondered whether they were walking on the ground; a young man and his girl; she dark-haired and pretty, with high color in her cheeks; he tall, fair-haired, handsome, looking down at her protected in his arm's circle, and laughing, moving nearer to me.

I love you.

I love you.

Time passed. They talked on, but I didn't listen, as they were talking comfortably with each other. My mother a young girl strolled again, my father beside her.

We have to get back.

Are you cold?

Oh, no! But it's lonesome here.

It's getting dark.

They're waiting for us.

Don't worry.

I love you.

I love you.

From the failing light I judged it was time to go. I put the empty drink bottle back into the carton. Somewhere Death waited, white on a white horse, prompt for an appointment at half past any hour. The unflushed covey nestled hidden somewhere beyond the noise of my footsteps, and I thought if I had time I would go and find them and roust them out, just to see the lovely explosion, just to make a sound in this quiet place. But instead I turned back to the street, shifting my Dr. Peppers and the picture of the young man to the other side, hoping I would not be late to meet Rose.

ABOUT THE AUTHOR

KATIE LETCHER LYLE was born in Peking, China, where her parents were stationed while her father served in the U.S. Marine Corps. She received her early education in Virginia public schools. She holds a bachelor of arts degree from Hollins College and a master of arts from Johns Hopkins, and has done work toward a Ph.D. at Vanderbilt.

She is married to Royster Lyle, who is Secretary of the George C. Marshall Research Foundation. The Lyles make their home in Lexington, Virginia, and have a son, Cochran. Since 1963 Mrs. Lyle has taught English at Southern Seminary Junior College, Buena Vista, Virginia, where she is now chairman of the Liberal Arts division.

Katie Letcher Lyle has many avocations in addition to writing. While in graduate school she was a professional folksinger. She is also an excellent cook and writes a weekly food column for *The Roanoke Times*. A book of poems, *Lyrics of Three Women*, was published in 1964. *I Will Go Barefoot All Summer for You* is her first novel.